LINDALEE

Days at Camp Sugar Pine

Lindalee

outskirts
press

Outskirts Press, Inc.
http://www.outskirtspress.com

ISBN: 978-1-9772-0897-2

Cover Image by Lindalee

PRINTED IN THE UNITED STATES OF AMERICA

To all my life long friends
who helped me become the person I am.

CHAPTER 1

I SAT ON my bedroom rug in the middle of a pile of clothes, some clean, some dirty. All wrinkled.

'After a big breakfast, a healthy way to start the day, you may choose the following activities: canoeing, archery, swimming, hiking, field sports, horseback riding, or arts and crafts with your new friends.'

That sounded a lot more exciting than the mess lying around me. I dropped the camp handbook and picked up a white tube sock with a large hole in the heel. Well, this sock wasn't coming with me. Camp sure sounded better than packing. I had two suitcases to get together before dinner.

"Tracey, bring down all your dirty clothes. I'm putting a load in now!" called Mother from the kitchen.

I picked up my khaki colored hoodie. Yuk! Nasty! I tossed it onto the washing pile. There was always so much to do to get ready. And, I always forgot something.

Last summer, at Camp Ravenwood, I forgot to bring a second pair of Nikes. One pair should've been enough. Camp was only three weeks. But I left them out to dry, after getting them soaked, when I crossed the river and slipped on the rocks. The counselor told me later that it looked like a friendly neighborhood bear had taken them. Boy! That was dumb! I'm sure he wasn't my size!

For the rest of the camp trip, I had to wear flip-flops. I found them in 'Lost and Found'. I hate thongs. They hurt between my toes. At the end of two weeks, my toes were blistered.

I picked up the handbook. There were so many things on the list for me to pack. What they wanted me to bring wasn't exactly what I wanted to bring. Thermal underwear. Now, what was I going to do with that! This was supposed to be summer. The last time, I wore thermal underwear, was when Nancy Ann, Sarah, and I were in New York City at Sarah's apartment. But it was snowing then. And very cold.

And insect repellant! That stuff stinks! I'd rather have a few mosquito bites than smell like insecticide.

My pillow! I must take my own pillow. It's so much better than the ones at camp. I don't like pillows made of sponge. And it would be my luck to get a lumpy one!

And my new diary. Sarah gave it to me just

before she left for New York. I promised to write in it every day. At least, try to write every day. Sarah said I could keep track of all the valuable pieces of information that I would forget to tell her when we got back together after vacation. Besides, I could save on buying stamps. I wouldn't have to write her every day. Maybe, a letter once a week instead. We were not allowed to text. We couldn't bring our cell phones. Oh, my itching powder! You never know when it would come in handy. Not here...hmmm...I remember now! It was under the underwear.

And my digital wristwatch. I couldn't forget that! Daddy gave it to me for my birthday. It does everything. It can even wake me up playing, 'Yankee Doodle Dandy'.

On the third page of the handbook were the camp rules:

1. 'Wear only clean clothes. Two washing facilities were located on the camp grounds.'

I hate washing. I'm glad it's only for three weeks.

2. 'Permanently mark all your items.'
3. 'For safety, wear shoes at all times except when swimming.'

Guess I'd better, or I'll probably lose them again.

4.   'No smoking. No vaping.'

That's ridiculous! None of us would do that! That's for people who don't know any better.

5.   'No alcoholic beverages.'

That's even more ridiculous! Who wants to drink that nasty stuff. Once I sneaked a sip of Daddy's beer. All I got was a mouthful of foam. And what a bitter taste. Nothing like my Coke. Mother says I drink too much Coke, but I love Coke and if I have to watch my weight, the drink might as well be sugarless—so I am changing to Diet Coke.

6.   'No candy allowed. It attracts bears.'

Now why would bears want our candy? They're probably making that up so we won't bring junk food.

7.   'No gum.'
8.   'No eating in bungalows.'

No candy. No gum. No eating in bungalows. That's dumb! We could bring candy to Camp Ravenwood last summer.

9. 'No boys allowed in camp.'
10. 'No girls allowed in the boys' camp.'
11. 'Do not leave camp without an adult or an approved buddy.'

That could be a drag.

12. 'Sweep and clean bungalows before breakfast daily.'

Before breakfast? Daddy would love that one.

13. 'Use only good manners. No bad language.'

He would love that one even more.

14. 'You are responsible for your own gear.'
15. 'Wake-up call will be six-thirty. Lights out at nine.'

Six-thirty! I thought this was a vacation.

16. 'No picking of any plant life is allowed.'

So much for Nancy Ann pressing flowers.

17. 'No playing with the wild animals; no feeding the animals.'

Last year, I was able to sneak home a little garter snake in my jacket pocket. I had to let it go in our yard when Dad found out. We weren't supposed to play with the animals at Ravenwood either.

18. 'Everyone will follow established lines of authority and support the camp program. If not, you will be sent home at your parents' expense.'
19. ''Respect and Responsibility' is Camp Sugar Pine's motto.'
20. 'Enjoy. Have a good time at Camp Sugar Pine.'

I groaned. Rules. There were so many rules for everything I did. I get them at home, school, and now, camp.

Well, I guess I'd better...

The phone cut into my thoughts. "I've got it, Mom!"

"Hi! Are you packed?"

It was Nancy Ann. My very best friend.

"Almost... but these rules, Nancy Ann. Did you read them? It seems like there are more and more rules every year."

"Depressing, isn't it?"

"Summer camp is supposed to be fun."

"Yeah, and we can't even have candy!"

"I sure...sure would like to sneak some," my voice lowered, "even, if it is bad for our faces."

There was silence. My mind was working overtime.

"Tracey, I know what we can do." Nancy Anne's voice reached one of her high-pitched notes. I wondered if her voice would ever change as she got older. Boys' voices do. But Nancy Ann wouldn't be Nancy Ann without her high voice.

"Our sleeping bags are already nice and lumpy. We could put candy in them. No one would even know the difference."

I've got to hand it to Nancy Ann. She could be as clever as me at times. Usually, I'm the one who comes up with the ideas. Especially, the sneaky ones.

"Royal's Market is having a four-for-one-dollar sale on candy," said Nancy Ann.

Hmmm...That was a good deal. Not much time though. I looked over at my alarm clock. Four-thirty.

"It's not going to be easy getting candy into the house. Dad's working in the yard. I'll talk to you tonight."

"Okay..... bye," and Nancy Ann hung up.

I looked at the mess around me, grabbed a pile of dirty laundry and one five-dollar bill that my Dad had given me to spend at camp and headed downstairs. Royal's Market, here I come.

Twenty minutes after reading Sugar Pine Camp's handbook, I was breaking rule number six.

CHAPTER 2

"TRACEY, HURRY UP!" I carried two suit-cases, my sleeping bag, and a pillow. I hoped my feet would find each step.

"You could have made two trips. Did you forget anything?" asked Mother.

"Probably," I replied.

Dad honked the horn. Either he was impatient or I was late. I dropped my things at the bottom of the stairs and looked at the grandfather clock. I was late.

"You're out of shape, Tracey. Hope summer camp gets you together. I understand they have a great physical fitness program... every day before breakfast."

"Before breakfast! Oh well, I'll just work up an appetite."

"But only for good food. Camp Sugar Pine is known for their Nutrition Program. You're going to have healthy meals of fruits and vegetables rather than junk food. Maybe, they can hammer some nutritional sense into that head of yours, since you don't listen to your Dad or me.

I thought about the candy bars rolled up in my sleeping bag and then dropped it for the second time. "My A's cap!" I almost forgot it. I ran up the steps two at a time.

"Oh, Tracey. Please hurry. The camp bus will leave without you."

As we pulled into the parking lot, I saw that I wasn't the only one late.

Nancy Ann looked like she had just gotten up. Her curly red hair was tousled from sleep. It was obvious, she hadn't combed it. I wondered if she had taken the time to brush her teeth. I hoped so.

"My alarm didn't go off."

"You mean, you forgot to set it. Did you eat breakfast?"

"No, but mother bagged a large lunch for me. I got enough for you, too."

"Well, are you two ready for the next three weeks?" asked Daddy.

"I guess so." I thought of the candy stuffed in my bag. After what Mom had just said about camp, I wondered if it was enough.

"I am." said Nancy Ann sleepily, "I stayed up late packing."

"Did you bring your Dre Beats?"

"Yeah, I packed them in my large suitcase in between my pajamas and hoodies. That should protect them."

"I didn't know you girls were allowed to bring Dre Beats to camp."

"Well, they didn't let us last year. But there was nothing in the rules about it this year, Dad. We're only going to play it in our cabin. Gosh, can you imagine three weeks without any music?"

"No, I can't image," Dad laughed. I bet he was going to miss me and my music. It was going to be awfully quiet around the house.

Twenty minutes later, Nancy Ann and I were still standing in the parking lot – baggage in hand, along with thirty-three other girls, waiting for the bus driver to stick our suitcases and bags in the bus storage area. Looking around, I recognized only one girl from last year's camp.

"Teressa. Hey T, over here." Teressa didn't like her name, so everyone called her T. It fit her perfectly. T was tall and slim with big brown eyes and warm brown skin. Her black hair hung down to her waist in ringlets.

"Hi, Tracey. Hi, Nancy Ann." T struggled up to us, arms loaded down with baggage.

"What a large sleeping bag!" Exclaimed Nancy Ann.

"Yeah, Mother got it for me this last week. It's made of down feathers. So soft. Wait till you lie on it."

"Hurry up, girls. Bring your bags over here."

The bus driver motioned to us with her large arms.

"Come on, T. Join us."

"Thanks. I don't know anyone else here. Wait....look, there's Robin!"

"Robin, over here." yelled Nancy Ann.

Nancy Ann and I had met Robin two years ago at summer camp. She was teased a lot because she was so tiny and rather shy. Robin was easy to be with. She went along with whatever we did.

"Hi guys."

"Well, we have half of our bungalow now. Wonder who will be the other four?" I asked.

July 7

Dear Sarah,

Just a letter to let you know that Nancy Ann and I have arrived at Camp Sugar Pine. There's room for eight of us in our bungalow. We have two of our bunk-mates already. Wish you were here. We miss you even though you've been gone only four days.

I can tell you now, I don't like saying good-byes. Coming back from the airport wasn't any fun. Your Mom did take us out for a Sundae, though, to make us feel better.

Of course, Nancy Ann had just about everything you could think of on hers as it was swimming in chocolate. Disgusting, as usual.

Hope your flight was good. At least, you didn't have to sit next to Nancy Ann holding a barf bag in her lap.

Speaking of barf bags, guess who gets sick on the camp bus? You're right. Nancy Ann. There were so many curves going up into the mountains. The bus driver told Nancy Ann to hang her head out the window and breathe in the fresh air. Luckily, Nancy Ann didn't eat her breakfast this morning. I don't think the bus driver believed me when I told her Nancy Ann gets car sick. Anyway, the window business didn't work and of course, there was no bathroom.

The bus finally took one curve too many and Nancy Ann upchucked. What a mess! She missed the window and hit the back of the seat and floor. The bus driver slammed on the brakes. Boy, was she mad!

Nancy Ann and I had to move to other seats, closer to the front. Closer to the bus driver. Ugh! Not only was she not very nice, but she smelled badly. I'm glad she's not one of our counselors. Wouldn't that be awful to have a mean counselor?

Anyway, the ride took three hours. Poor Nancy Ann. She was so miserable. She couldn't eat the lunch that her Mother packed for her. But it didn't go to waste. T, Robin, and I ate it. T and Robin are our bunkmates.

It's too late to mail this letter today. But I'll get it in tomorrow's mail. I promise. That was a great idea of yours giving me that diary. I will write all the details of our camp experiences in it, and you will be able to read about them when we all get together.

"Tracey, come on. The chow bell is ringing. I'm starving," Nancy Ann said smiling.

"I'm coming. Give me a minute."

Bye Sarah. I'll write to you in my diary tomorrow. Hope things are okay between you and your DAD. XOX Tracey

CHAPTER 3

"TRACEY, THAT HAD to be the 'AWFULEST' meal ever. I hate cabbage! And on top of it, it was stuffed!"

"Yeah, but stuffed with what?" asked T, who was walking next to Nancy Ann and me.

"Beans, rice, and eggs," I said.

"Remember, this is supposed to be good for us!" said Robin. "It may make me grow," she laughed.

"But why rhubarb pudding?" I groaned. Rhubarb makes my stomach feel funny. Especially, mixed with wheat germ.

"That's supposed to be good for our digestive systems," said Nancy Ann shrugging. "That's what the cook told me."

"Hey look! Our door is open! I thought we closed it." Nancy Ann's voice quivered on a high note.

An overhead light glared through the open door. I bent down and picked up a crumpled piece of paper. A candy wrapper!

"I'm not going in there!" declared Nancy Ann.

"Neither am I," said T.

I've always been the one with the most guts, but this time I felt I was getting into something bigger than what I was used to.

"Go in, Tracey." whispered Nancy Ann.

Why me? I thought, as I pushed the door open wider with my foot.

Wow! What a mess!

Everything was everywhere, along with pieces of candy wrappers. My bag was ripped to shreds, but it was old and I knew I wouldn't get in too much trouble. T started crying. Her nice sleeping bag was gutted and feathers were everywhere.

"It's all your fault!" cried T. Some animal had invaded our home. "You had candy, didn't you?" Before I could answer, our bungalow was pounced upon by Brenda.

Unknown to us, two girls from the bungalow next door had gone to get a counselor. They had bumped right into Brenda, the number one camp counselor.

"What's going on here?" a voice boomed behind me.

July 8

Dear Diary,

What a way to begin camp memories! Bungalow fourteen, (that's us) was broken into tonight. Either by a bear or bears, or some other animal according to our counselor. All that was left, after the animal had gone, were pieces of sleeping bags and torn candy wrappers.

Things wouldn't have been so bad, but two girls from next door became frantic when they walked in behind us. Those tattletales. I bet no one likes them at school.

Anyway, Nancy Ann and I ended up at the Camp Director's office. We got chewed out but good. She said we placed our bungalow in a dangerous situation. Bears could attack if people get in the way of the food they want. And bears like sweets. The Director said we were fortunate not to have been inside the bungalow.

"Tracey, turn off the flashlight. It's keeping me awake!" said Nancy Ann.

"Shhh" said T angrily.

"Sorry, give me another minute."

Besides cleaning up the mess – and it was a mess, Nancy Ann and I had to make three beds without the sleeping bags, and starting tomorrow, Nancy Ann and I are on bathroom duty for the whole week. All for bringing in a bag...

"Tracey!"

"Okay." I clicked off the flashlight. I would finish my entry later. But I wanted to write most of it tonight, as I might not have time tomorrow. According to Brenda, our day will be full. Besides early morning activities, there are four large bathroom-shower areas in the camp. What a nightmare! Cleaning up a bathroom in a house has to be the nastiest job, let alone four of them in a girls' camp.

CHAPTER 4

"WHAT'S THAT?" NANCY Ann's voice sounded muffled. She must've had her head under her pillow. My eyelids stayed closed.

"I'm not sure." I mumbled.

The noise continued.

"That's the bugle." T said. "It goes off every morning at six-thirty."

"But my watch hasn't even gone off yet. They're early." At that moment, 'Yankee Doodle Dandy' sounded. I put my pillow over my head.

"That means exercising and then showering," groaned Nancy Ann.

"Everyone up!" said T as she jumped down from a top bunk.

"But it's too early!" whined Nancy Ann.

How can anyone get up this early? Staying in bed was a much better idea than the day I had ahead of me. Bathroom duty. Ugh!

"Ladies, you have ten minutes to get yourselves together for aerobics class!" Brenda's voice boomed loud and clear.

"I don't think I like that voice!" I said, my eyes still shut.

The bungalow door opened and the screen door slammed. "Well, what do we have here? Four sleeping beauties?"

"No, just three. I'm up." said T.

"Well, you look like groundhogs to me. In fact, that's a good name for your group. You'll be the Groundhogs. Now, up and at'em. Report to morning exercise and then the showers!"

I threw off the army blanket and extended a leg over the edge of the upper bunk. Climbing down is not as easy as climbing up.

"Hey!"

My foot landed on something soft.

"Oh, sorry, Nancy Ann. What's your hand doing there?"

"It's attached to my body and my body is lying in this bunk!"

Nancy Ann is not an early morning person. But neither am I.

I grabbed my soap, toothpaste, brush, and towel for showering later on. "Come on, let's go. Come on, Robin. Get up!"

Brenda was outside yelling at another group of girls. Lucky for us, the exercise knoll was only minutes away.

Later on while I brushed my teeth, I reflected on our exercise regimen. I looked in the mirror and saw the open shower. Mildew blackened the corners of the stall. I hated cleaning the bath, especially after other people. I could imagine all kinds of germs and bugs crawling everywhere.

I splashed water on my face without taking the time to let it get warm. So, I got a face full of cold mountain water. Well, if this doesn't wake me up, nothing will, I thought.

Someone grabbed at the ties of my robe. "Let's go, Tracey. Brenda will be here in a minute," said Nancy Ann.

As it was, Brenda waited for us outside, "Breakfast and then your bathroom duty!"

"Tracey," whispered Nancy Ann, sounding a bit annoyed. "Where did your mother hear about Camp Sugar Pine?"

"I don't know. I've wondered about that myself. Perhaps, from one of her health magazines." I also thought about this as we were doing or stretching exercises.

"Okay, ladies. Let's stretch those muscles. Reach high. Grab onto the sky. Now bend down. Can your fingers touch the ground?" Brenda's voice bounced back and forth in my ears.

My knees buckled and my butt crumpled to the ground. "Ohhh. I'm not going to live through this, Nancy Ann."

"Oh, I see one of the Groundhogs is not going to make it!" yelled Brenda.

I winced. I've never seen a drill sergeant in action before, but I've heard about them. I wondered where Brenda did her training. I pulled myself up. I'll show her, I thought.

"Feel your stomach tighten."

All I could feel was my empty stomach. Last night's dinner had been far from satisfying.

Mother was right. I must be out of shape. Thirty minutes of exercise was twenty minutes too long. Both Nancy Ann and I collapsed on the grass as we tucked our legs under our fannies for the last time.

"Let's go, Tracey. We need to shower."

"All I can think about are banana pancakes floating in syrup." commented Nancy Ann.

"I have a feeling you are dreaming. Especially after last night's dinner. We'll probably have cottage cheese floating in crushed fruit. But at the moment, I can eat anything."

"Well, you're right about the fruit, Tracey." As we looked onto the trays of food sitting on the tables.

"Yeah, but cheese and apples, and lumpy oatmeal. Yuck!"

"It's not all that bad. It could be worse."

"Worse?" asked Nancy Ann.

"Yeah, it's only for three weeks. Not a lifetime."

"That's true, but right now it seems like a lifetime," laughed Nancy Ann.

"Well, I'm glad you two are so happy. Hurry up and finish that oatmeal. You have work to do!" Brenda's voice was demanding.

"I'm full," I said.

"Me too," said Nancy Ann, her voice rising shrilly.

"Finish it! It's good for you," snapped Brenda.

"Boy, she's worse than a mother," whispered T from the other side of me.

"More like a drill sergeant!"

"What did you say?" boomed Brenda's voice.

I looked up at Brenda's moon-shaped face staring back at me. It matched the rest of her body, overgrown and powerful.

"I just asked Nancy Ann if she was ready to get to work."

"And what did Nancy Ann say?"

I cut in, "She asked me if we had a choice."

Nancy Ann's face grimaced. Inside, I laughed.

"Smarty pants, huh?" Let's go. You have some hard hours of work ahead of you," said Brenda, smiling.

"I don't like her smile, Tracey."

"I don't like her face."

"Ditto," replied Nancy Ann as we walked behind Brenda out of the chow hall door. As we left the hall, the entire room rocked with talk and laughter.

As we walked into one of the bathrooms, graffiti stood out all over the walls.

"Tracey, I get no thrills from reading graffiti."

"Some of it is pretty good. Really creative. But, it's not so much fun cleaning it off the tile walls."

"Ugh, and some of the words people use."

"Look! Nancy Ann, it must be a thing here to throw toilet paper on the ceiling just like it is back at school. Now, how are we going to reach it?"

"Want to climb on my shoulders?" Nancy Ann smirked.

"I think we'll use a ladder."

The next three hours were spent with Lysol in one hand and a sponge in the other: scrubbing floors, sinks, walls, and toilets while wearing much-too-large rubber gloves. The worse job was unplugging two bowls stuffed with paper. I had my fill of bathrooms. I didn't say anything as we walked back to our own shower stalls. I had a feeling that 'Big B', as Nancy Ann and I had renamed Brenda, was watching us, following our movements with her constant sadistic smile.

Later, I felt a lot better as we headed to our bungalow.

"Tracey, you must've stepped in something because there's a bunch of junk attached to your shoe."

I lifted my shoe. Gum! I had stepped on a big wad of gum! Yuck! Some people! They can be so nasty, throwing their trash around. No wonder one of the camp rules was no chewing gum. I guess sometimes there are good reasons for having rules. I just wondered what life would be like without rules. Probably a bit chaotic. And messy.

CHAPTER 5

July 8

DEAR DIARY,

Well, I'm back, but not in very good shape, I'm afraid.

Nancy Ann is out on a hike with T and Robin. Don't know where Nancy Ann gets her energy 'cause I'm dead after this morning.

Smuggling candy into camp wasn't such a good idea after all. I have never worked so hard. The shower stalls were really yucky. 'Big B', that's for Brenda, is our overseer. Actually, she's our counselor. She watches over us like a hawk. Every move we make, she's right there. We didn't stop to think about what she would do to us if we had stopped cleaning the bathrooms. Her muscles rippled every time her eyebrows came together. And that's a lot!

We got the rest of our bunkmates. They just walked in. Rather three of them walked. Bambi rumbled in like a tidal wave. She's big. You would be nice and call her heavyset. She must be flat-footed 'cause her Nikes make a thudding noise every time she took a step.

The others are now discussing who gets which bunk. It's not easy writing to you with all this noise going on. Now, Bambi is in on the discussion.

Can you imagine, Bambi wanted the top bunk! Maybe, it makes her feel more important. You should've seen her climb up. And I thought I was clumsy. I remember when your Mom took us to that trapeze artist show that came to town. Well, I look like a trapeze artist next to Bambi trying to climb up to her bunk bed.

I wondered why she chose the top bunk. Maybe, it makes her feel more important.

I have the top bunk because Nancy Ann still doesn't like high places of any kind. It wasn't much of a decision.

One of the other girls, Heather, took the bunk under Bambi. She is the organized roommate.

Heather has already started unpacking and putting things away. She seems nice enough. But hasn't said a whole lot yet.

The other two, Helen and Candy, must be friends. They act like no one else is around. They didn't even say hi when they came in. Probably snobs. They even brought their own tennis rackets! I don't think Helen or Candy like the bungalow. They don't act like it...especially, the bunk beds. Not good enough for them, I suppose.

Speaking about bunk beds, T, Nancy Ann, and I are sleeping between folded double sheets with an army blanket on top. My blanket fell off the bunk last night. Was I ever frozen when I woke up. Nights are cold here. I might end up wearing my thermals yet. I miss my sleeping bag. Nancy Ann had no problem sleeping. She can sleep through anything and wherever. She almost slept through the bugle call.

That's how they get us up around here. A six-thirty bugle call, then aerobics and jogging for thirty minutes. And boy, I'm not ready for that. My body aches from all the exercise and the awful bathroom clean-up. The camp brochure talked about all the fresh air, great outdoors, and well-planned, healthy meals. Such fun, such excitement.

They misnamed Camp Sugar Pine. Speaking of sugar, what sugar? It's remarkable how many things can be made with very little sugar, salt, and fat. We're just finding out. They have three square meals, and I mean square, planned- out meals for us each day. I missed lunch. After three hours of bathroom duty, I had no desire to sit through lunch.

One thing for sure, I bet I lose weight. I can't overload on this food.

More later. My hand is tired. Between scrubbing and writing, my fingers feel numb.

CHAPTER 6

"TRACEY, COME WITH us. Hiking is fun. It's really beautiful here," said Nancy Ann excitedly.

"How far do we have to walk?" I still felt pain from the top of my head on down. My muscles screamed. The second day's workout hadn't helped. But the bathrooms weren't so bad today since Nancy Ann and I had really scrubbed them down yesterday.

"We don't walk. It's more like climbing!"

I groaned. "When do we have to be ready?"

"T's ready now. Heather and Robin are going too. Let's go to the canteen and get some food to take with us."

"Like raisins and nuts?" That's about all you'll find there. Maybe, an apple or orange or more rabbit food?"

"Come on. That's not so bad."

Nancy Ann was right. The mountains were beautiful. The tallest trees looked down on us. I'd never seen anything so tall. And the woods were full of sounds. Mostly birds, cawing and singing.

"What kinds of trees are these?" I asked, my neck straining upwards. Oh, that hurt.

"I read all about them yesterday," said Heather. "See those? They are the Giant Sequoias. They are the largest trees on earth today! Sometimes they're so big, that one Giant Sequoia can have more wood in it than can be found on a few acres of good timberland."

"Well, listen to her," said T as she pulled the knuckles on her right hand.

She always sounds that way, I thought. She has something to say about everything.

"You're just jealous!" snapped Heather, "because I know a lot of things."

"Hey, you two. Stop it! There's nothing wrong with knowing about things. I read all the time. Ask Tracey."

"Nancy Ann's right. She reads more than anyone I know. Except my Dad. But that doesn't count. He went to college."

"Reading opens all kinds of doors to other areas of life. Heather, tell us more about Sequoias," said Nancy Ann, "they're mammoth!"

"Well..." Heather just looked at T and then back at Nancy Ann. "Their trunks can grow up to fifteen feet in diameter and they can reach two hundred and fifty feet in height."

They sure are impressive, I thought. The trees reminded me of the buildings we had seen in New York. But these were not man-made.

"Look, there's one that has fallen over!"

Robin ran to the tree.

"Look! I can stand up inside of it!"

Nancy Ann and I laughed. "Your voice echoes, too."

T sang a line from the song, 'One Hundred Bottles of Beer on the Wall'.

We laughed as we all managed to squeeze inside. "See, I told you they can get big," said Heather.

"Their nickname is 'Big Tree'".

"I can see why," T commented. "But it's pretty tight in here."

"Here we are at Camp Sugar Pine and all we see are Giant Sequoias. Where are the Sugar Pines?" asked T.

Everyone fell silent. I looked at Heather. "Well?" I said.

"See. That tree over there? And that one? That one is a Sugar Pine. They get really tall, too," said Heather. "In fact, they're the tallest and largest of the world's more than one hundred different kinds of pine trees." T groaned.

"Why are they called Sugar Pines?" asked Nancy Ann as we all walked over to the first one Heather had pointed to.

"See those large pine cones hanging from the branches? Well, the nuts from the cones were harvested by the Native Americans. The sugary, sticky sap was also a special treat for them. It comes from the trunk of the tree and it's like our maple syrup. But you can't eat very much of it 'cause it makes you go to the bathroom."

"Bathroom! Does that remind you two of anything?" asked T. Everyone laughed. T could be so annoying. Not having seen T since last summer, I had forgotten why I had not texted her during the school year. She was just plain irritating. T liked to egg people on and make people uncomfortable. Neither Nancy Ann or I, answered her.

A squirrel dashed in front of us and we all stopped talking at once. It scampered over to a Sugar Pine cone lying on the ground. It began ripping off the cone's scales. We stood and watched as he carefully picked off the nuts, pocketing them all in his mouth.

"Look what he's doing!" said Robin.

"Shhh...! I said.

At the sound of Robin's voice, the squirrel stopped, turned around to look at us, and scampered off.

"Did he eat all those nuts?" Asked T.

"Don't be silly," said Heather. "They're all in his cheeks. He'll go bury them somewhere. When winter comes, he'll get hungry and then dig them up. Hopefully, he will remember where he hid them."

"Well, I guess we all learned a few things today," said Nancy Ann. "See there's nothing wrong with learning. Either from a book or from someone else. Or simply experiencing it."

"Come on, let's go. This area is too big to stay in one spot very long," I said.

"Isn't the boys' camp in this direction?" asked Nancy Ann.

"Yeah, but remember, Camp Bigfoot is definitely off limits," stated Heather.

"But it wouldn't hurt to walk in that direction," I said. "In fact, that's a good direction to go. Come on."

"Tracey, have you ever thought of taking up custodial care of the bathrooms. Permanently?"

Another one of T's side remarks.

"Well, let's walk around to the other side of Sugar Pine Lake, at least," said Nancy Ann.

"You can always be her assistant," said T, and everyone laughed.

"I might have known there would be more to this hike than just Mother Nature," said Heather flatly as we trudged along a well-worn trail that led to Camp Bigfoot.

"Well, I've been wanting to see Sugar Pine Lake anyway," I remarked. "I would like to go boating sometime this week."

"Yeah, me too." Commented Robin.

"I'm not sure how close we can get to the boys' camp without getting ourselves into trouble," said Nancy Ann, whispering.

Everyone's voice started getting lower. A

sure sign that we must be getting nearer to Camp Bigfoot. I breathed in deeply, hoping it would calm my nerves. All we needed to do was to get into trouble again.

Rule number ten, here we go.

CHAPTER 7

I'M GOING TO be a mass of scratches and bruises, I thought, as I crawled on my knees and ducked my head to avoid being mauled by a very sticky bush. Why had I opened my mouth? Going to Camp Bigfoot wasn't worth all of our trouble. None of us had said very much in the last ten minutes. Even the birds seemed quiet. My jacket caught on a low-hanging branch. I yanked hard.

Rip...... oh, oh, I thought. I could hear Daddy now, "Tracey, you didn't take very good care of your things – first your sleeping bag and then your down jacket."

"I'm hungry, Tracey!" said Nancy Ann.

"Yeah, me too," I said.

"How much further do we have to go?" whined T, "I'm tired of crawling on my knees and jumping from rock to rock. I'm not made for all this country living."

"We should be almost there," I said, sounding annoyed. "Where is your sense of adventure? If you're going to complain, stay home next time. I have a bag of sunflower seeds. That should hold you over till we get back to camp."

"I have a package of raisins," said Nancy Ann.

I felt in my pocket for my apple. Well, I guess it was better than nothing.

"Here, take a bite, Nancy Ann."

"And I've been holding myself for the past twenty minutes," said T, "and that doesn't do my bladder any good!"

"OMG!" blurted out Heather loudly. I laughed. Nancy Ann stifled a giggle.

I was glad I hadn't opened my mouth to complain.

"Shhh! Someone will hear you." I whispered.

"Look! Through those trees!" Nancy Ann pointed to the top of a log cabin type building.

Something like the one I imagined Abe Lincoln was born in.

"That must be the boys' camp!" said T.

"Look, there are more cabins through those trees!"

"Do you see any guys?" asked Robin.

Smoke curled lazily upward. It ran right into a group of darkening clouds.

"No, but look!" I said as I straightened myself out, pulling sticker burrs out of the sleeve of my jacket.

"Clouds!" Nancy Ann's voice cracked.

"And they don't look inviting! Let's get out

of here!" stammering T, pulling at her knuckles.
"I'm not dressed for rain."

"Neither are we!" chimed Heather and
Robin.

"Tracey, your idea was a flop! Not only are
we hungry and tired, but we're going to get wet!"
whined Nancy Ann.

"Yep, I would say in about ten minutes," said
Heather assuredly.

I don't like being around people who are
always right but this time, I knew Heather was
right. As I looked up at the clouds, a drop of water
fell smack dab on the center of my forehead.

I looked at the faces of my four comrades.
There was no way I could describe them to Sarah
in my diary.

Things could be worse, I thought. We could
be caught in a blizzard or a hurricane. Why
couldn't people have a positive attitude like
mine?

I zipped up my jacket and pulled the collar
up around my ears. I was cold and I shivered.

"Let's see if we can get back to camp faster
than we got here," I suggested, a smile forced
upon my face. "Come on, the first one back is the
first one in the chow line!"

"That's not much of an incentive," groaned
Nancy Ann. "Unless you are a rabbit!"

I didn't mind smiling, but I didn't feel like
laughing, so I pretended I didn't hear Nancy

Ann's comment. If we were lucky, we could get back to camp in thirty minutes. But luck didn't seem to be with us today.

I licked a scratch on my hand and turned back in the direction of Camp Sugar Pine. Disaster struck. It was as if the clouds opened up a trap door and poured out all the water at once.

Buckets and buckets of water. A cloudburst.

All of us got drenched within minutes. My Nikes squished, squashed, picking up pine needles as I slipped and slid, trying to keep my balance.

Nancy Ann whimpered. Robin muttered words I couldn't hear under her breath.

"Well, if this isn't just dandy!" complained T.

I didn't say anything. I was wondering if I still wanted to be an adventurer. I concentrated on the path back to camp. All the trees looked the same – tall and scary. There were no footsteps to follow. Wet pine needles covered the ground. If only I was part Native-American I thought, we would already be back at camp. I knew T really had to go to the bathroom now. Every time I was around water, I always had to go. Daddy said it was all in my head. It had to do with psychology or something like that.

And I knew it was getting late. Yankee Doodle Dandy doodled five o'clock.

Robin sneezed. I hoped that didn't mean that she was catching a cold. She didn't need that.

We might all come down with colds. I was so wet.

Nancy Ann nudged me. "Tracey," she whispered. "Are you sure we're going in the right direction?"

I paused. "No, but I'm hoping we are." Nancy Ann didn't say anything.

Why can't life be easy, I thought, with only straight lines and no curves. My life was filled with so many curves. And walls seemed to be around every corner. Often, I turned too quickly and too many times. I brought my friends with me. Like this afternoon.

Thank goodness for the Giant Sequoia. Heather's idea to find shelter till the rain let up was a good one. It had become so dark with all the clouds and rain that we couldn't see very far ahead of us. Off to the side of the trail was a burned-out hollow of a Sequoia. We ran for cover.

My jacket wasn't enough. The dampness had crawled up inside it. Oh, how I wished we were back up at camp in some warm, dry clothes.

"Tracey, do you think they have missed us yet?" whispered Nancy Ann.

"I hope not," I said. I could see Big B right now, with her smirking smile, thinking that this served us right for going off without checking out. If she knew where we had gone to, we would really be in trouble.

CHAPTER 8

DEAR DIARY,

I can barely move my fingers. My body is stiff and my joints are numb.

Nancy Ann, T, Heather, Robin, and I went on a hike. Bambi was smart and didn't go. Thank goodness for us. When we didn't show up an hour after a cloudburst hit, she reported us missing to the Camp Director.

It didn't take long for the search party to find us. Big B must have a nose for direction. Either that, or other girls before had wandered off in the direction of the boys' camp. She found us all bundled up in the hollow of a burned-out tree trunk.

I know I'm sick. Not from just being out in the storm, but from Big B. She blamed the whole incident on Nancy Ann and me. I don't know how she came to that conclusion. Nancy Ann thinks she has it in for us. We're the only ones that get in trouble.

Nancy Ann and I almost got another week of bathroom duty. The only thing that saved us was that Mrs. Scarfield, the Camp Director, felt sorry for us. She sent us to bed with a bowl of cream of celery soup. None of us are feeling so good.

Robin is the most miserable. They gave us extra blankets to keep warm, but I'm still having chills. I think I'm running a high temperature but am afraid to ask for a thermometer for fear of it breaking. Besides, I really don't want to know if I'm dying or not. I am now wearing my thermal underwear.

The soup was gross looking. Pieces of stringy celery stalks floated on top of a milky white substance. I'm not particularly fond of soup. All it does is fill me up and there's no space for anything else. I gave my soup to Nancy Ann. She eats anything.

Bambi had made me a sandwich at the chow hall: slices of wheat toast packed *with lettuce, tomatoes, water chestnuts, cucumbers, sliced bell peppers, dill pickles, and bean sprouts. Then she poured yogurt salad dressing in between. It was a bit soggy 'cause it was wrapped in two napkins, but it tasted pretty good. I was hungry. Even the bean sprouts were okay and I hate beans. In fact, they didn't taste at all like beans. They looked like worms. I just closed my eyes and stuffed my mouth.*

Bambi was getting me some cranberry aspic, whatever that is but she ended up eating it. No wonder she's overweight. She can't stop eating. Oh well, the thought was there. She really is nice. I do like her.

Bambi's aunt is a nurse, so Bambi is now an expert on sick people. She said it looks like we all have colds except for Heather. She just has the sniffles. Heather never gets colds. At least, that's what she tells us. Anyway, Bambi has taken everyone's temperature but mine, gotten us some fruit juice, and is playing the role of a nurse. I bet she would like to be a nurse like her aunt. Maybe, this is her training ground since we're her first patients.

Gosh, I feel terrible. My head aches too.

It's still raining outside, but not as badly as before. Once I saw the sky light up. There's lightning in the distance. The thunder is far off. I hope it doesn't get closer.

I don't mind lightning, but thunder makes me jump. I'm never ready for the noise.

And if that's not enough bad news, now that it's raining, we are stuck inside with Helen and Candy. Boy, are they drips, especially when I'm not feeling well. I wonder why they're even here. The best I can figure, their parents sent them to camp to get rid of them. If they aren't playing tennis, they're no good to anyone.

The other half of the time, they sit in front of their portable make-up mirror with battery powered lights fixing their faces. Mother would kill me if I put on that junk.

Must be a tough life to be rich and allowed to do anything you want to.

July 10

Couldn't wait till tonight to write. The

dumbest thing happened last night. Would you believe a fire drill? At four-thirty in the morning! We all had to line up outside while they counted heads. They said it was for our own safety. "One never knows when there will be a real fire," said Mrs. Scarfield. They could've picked a better night to do it. Half of the camp is sick.

Well, at least half of our bungalow. Robin refused to go on the drill. For being so little, she has a lot of spunk. Big B had to come in to get her. It was only drizzling, but puddles were everywhere. And it was dark. There was no dry ground anywhere and I got wet up to my knees. Robin was even wetter. Being so tiny.

The two that complained the most were Candy and Helen, and they're not even sick. Something to do with their beauty sleep I suppose.

Those two are really into this camp – they're gung ho about aerobics and the food.

I overheard them talking about some natural food recipes. Maybe, all of this is the reason they look so good. Anyway, being around them doesn't make me feel very positive about myself.

CHAPTER 9

"TRACEY, HOW DOES it feel to be on our last day of detail?" Huffed Nancy Ann as she swished a soapy mop across the cold cement floor.

"These past seven days have gone too slowly," I said. Actually, we had missed two days of scrubbing showers, thanks to Mrs. Scarfield. I don't know which was worse, cleaning toilet bowls or having the chills. "Maybe, Big B will leave us alone so we can have some fun."

"Yeah, I wouldn't mind getting up for jazzercise and jogging around the camp, knowing we can go swimming or horseback riding later. Everyone has been having a good time but us."

"Maybe, we can work on our tans too. My skin is so white I look like an albino. I sure would like to have a tan for the camp social Wednesday evening with the group from Camp Bigfoot coming over. I thought about the nice tans that Candy and Heather had already started. Maybe, a tan would make me look better. How much better I didn't know.

"Won't that be fun? I hope they're some nice-looking guys. Better than at school."

I thought about my friend Butch, wondering what he was doing. His family had gone up to Yellowstone for several weeks. He should be home now. He's nice looking for a boy, but nothing like Sarah's Father, who was so handsome. Maybe, Butch would grow into it.

"Tracey, what are you thinking about? Not about boys, I hope. Don't get your hopes up.

Mother says when you think too much about something, it never turns out like you want it to.

"Right now, all I'm thinking about is getting out of these grubby clothes, eating lunch, and going swimming. Maybe canoeing." I commented.

"Wow. Let's do that. I've never been canoeing. Robin and Heather went yesterday. In fact, everyone went except Bambi. I don't think she likes the water very much."

"Well, that's my last toilet. Let's go."

After leaning the mops in the corner, we took off our gloves and headed back to our own bungalow to clean up.

I had to admit my stomach was adjusting to the food. I guess you can get used to anything if you have to. Today's menu was lentil-mushroom stew. I concentrated on the mushrooms, picking them out one by one. Lentils were too much like beans. The salad bar saved me. I made a salad of several kinds of fruit.

Now, I really love fruit, but I don't eat it too often. Fruit has lots of sugar in it. I know because I have an uncle who is always watching his weight. He's always eating lots of salads and fruit. He says it's very good for you. But he is very big and getting bigger, and all he ever eats are salads and fruit. Maybe, it is the heavy salad dressing and all the sugar in fruit.

I finished off my bowl of fruit and cleaned up my table area. Big B stood by the door and glared at us as we left the chow hall.

"Stay out of trouble, girls. I don't have to remind you that you're on probation, Groundhogs."

She loved to call us that. I guess we were stuck with the name, but I wasn't going to let her bother me today.

"Where are you guys going?" asked T, running up behind us.

"We're going canoeing," said Nancy Ann in her high-pitched voice. Everyone decided to go. Everyone except Bambi, standing there with her sad, puppy dog eyes, looking like my idea of an underdog.

"Yesterday was lots of fun," said Robin, smearing a glob white creamy sunscreen lotion on her already pink nose. She wasn't taking any chances today. I just wanted some of that sun.

"I'm not sure...sure if one of those jackets can fit me," said Bambi. She was definitely playing the underdog.

"I bet we could find one for you." I started digging through the box of life preservers. I kept my fingers crossed as I searched for one. All small sizes. At the bottom, I saw a jacket with the name of Brenda printed on it.

"Here, this one should fit." I wanted Bambi to go with us. She needed to be included.

"Do you think so?" Bambi asked hopefully as she put her right arm through it. The jacket fit. I discovered a long time ago that positive thinking usually paid off. I just hoped she hadn't seen Brenda's name on it.

"Come on," said Heather impatiently. "We can't waste all that sunshine and water."

Heather gave us a two-minute lesson on the pros and cons of canoeing.

"And never, never stand up in the canoe."

Everyone knows that, I thought.

We divided into two groups, the canoes being pretty long. Bambi came with Nancy Ann and me. At first, I thought the canoe would sink below the water line as Bambi got into it, but with Nancy Ann's weight and mine to offset Bambi's, everything turned out okay.

"We couldn't have planned a better day," commented Bambi, meekly peering into the sun. I could tell she was happy being with us.

"On a scale from one to ten, it's an A plus," said Nancy Ann, laughing.

"Remember, push the paddles on opposite

sides or you'll keep turning around in a circle," said Heather sharply. I bet Heather will be a teacher when she gets older. She fits the image perfectly.

We paddled for almost an hour. My arms were getting pretty tired.

"Let's stop for a five-minute break," I said.

"Good idea," said Nancy Ann.

Soon, our canoe drifted into some low-hanging tree branches that leaned far out over the water.

"Yesterday, we heard that a monster is supposed to live in the lake," said T.

Heather laughed. "That's only a made-up story. I think the health food here is affecting your brain."

"Maybe, but several of the girls were talking about it," said Robin curtly.

I shivered. Sometimes, there was fact where there was fiction. "Let's paddle away from these straggly branches," I said.

"Yeah. It probably lives in those bushes over there," said Heather smirking.

"No, it's supposed to live in the middle of the lake, said T, adamantly.

Then her face turned red.

"Maybe, a change of scenery?" I asked. "A little more action maybe? This lake is not much of a challenge." I didn't feel like running into that lake monster.

"Well, Sugar Pine Lake is really a dammed-up part of the river, so maybe we could explore that," said T.

"I don't think that is on our list of things we can do," said Bambi, hesitantly.

"She's right," said Heather.

"Come on, don't be such chickens. Who will find out? There's no one here, but us. Besides, we can actually paddle somewhere there. This lake goes nowhere," I said.

Nancy Ann and I dipped our paddles into the water. Bambi did the same. The other canoe followed.

"This is better," I said. "At least, we are going somewhere."

Sprays of water fanned me.

"Nancy Ann, this is great!"

"Tracey, it feels like we're going faster than we should. I don't have to paddle very hard."

"Me either." I didn't like how fast we were going, but I wasn't going to worry Nancy Ann by telling her my fears.

"Can't we slow this thing down?" asked Bambi.

"I'm not sure how to do it," I said.

It's amazing how fast a canoe can move. Especially, when you're scared.

Not that I was. But I was getting there. The water seemed choppier and the spray had turned into white foam bouncing off our canoe. Maybe, this was not such a good idea after all.

I looked back. Heather yelled something to us, but I couldn't hear her. Water can be very noisy. Both Nancy Ann and Bambi were holding on to the sides of the canoe. Nancy Ann looked pale. All I could see were her freckles. I was wet and I just knew I was going to get wetter.

CHAPTER 10

"HEY BAMBI, QUIT rocking the canoe!" I yelled.

"That's not me!"

"She's not lying!" shrieked Nancy Ann. "The boat feels like it's splitting apart!"

Up ahead, the rushing water careened in every direction.

"Look at those rocks!" shouted Bambi.

"Those are boulders!" whined Nancy Ann, her voice straining.

I now knew why canoeing on the river was off limits. The white foamy water seemed to come up faster and faster.

I grabbed my paddle more tightly. Our canoe lurched and swept down around the boulders. Someone cried out behind me. I didn't have time to look around. Just in front of us the water swirled into a whirlpool.

Yikes...what's next? I thought.

"I'm going to be sick!" wailed Nancy Ann. Our canoe spun around. This was worse than the Ferris Wheel. At least, you knew when it was going to stop.

"Bambi, sit down!" screamed Nancy Ann. Just as I turned around, Bambi went over the side, tipping the canoe over.

Cold, cold water instantly saturated my clothes.

"Nancy Ann are you..." I lost all my words in a mouthful of water. I pulled all of my strength and determination together and headed for one of the rocks.

Thank God for being a good swimmer. Dad had me in the water when I was three insisting that I learn how to swim.

I think I pulled every muscle in my right arm heading for the shallow water. The current was going strong. The water was calmer when I got there. I touched the rocky bottom with my Nikes. I was glad I was wearing them. It made it much easier to stand.

"Nancy Ann, over here." The other canoe was right behind.

"Hang on you guys!" yelled Heather. Their canoe had reached us. T was bent over the edge of the canoe holding on to Bambi. In Brenda's bright orange life jacket, she bobbed up and down.

"Oh, Tracey, this is too much. I'd settle for a swim in a pool anytime," said Nancy Ann.

A sense of humor is a great asset to have, especially in times of trouble.

Nancy Ann was a good friend.

"Is everyone okay?" asked Robin. "Grab hold of my paddle, Nancy Ann."

Someone had thrown a life saver nearby and Nancy Ann grabbed it even though she had her life vest on.

"Hold on and we'll pull you to shore," said Heather calmly.

Minutes later, three soaked girls sat on the rocky shore.

I just couldn't catch cold again, I thought. My whole time at camp would be spent either in bed or on my knees cleaning bathrooms. Oh, why me?

"I'm so cold," shivered Nancy Ann.

"Yeah, me too," said Bambi, softly.

"I want to go back to camp and get dry," whimpered Nancy Ann.

I looked at the overturned canoe. It was caught on the rocks at the edge of the whirlpool. One of us is going to get wet again. I looked at my two friends. Well, this was sort of my idea, so I guess it's on me.

I waded into the water and grabbed the canoe, pulling hard. The current was strong, but I had more determination.

Now six girls sat on the shore, three of them shaking in their wet clothes.

"Well, looks like we walk back," said Heather. "And it's going to take us a while, especially carrying those canoes."

"We'd better start soon," said Nancy Ann, "before Big B comes looking for us."

"She's right," I said. "I don't' feel like getting into trouble again."

"How long do you think it will take us to get back?" asked Bambi. Her puppy dog eyes seemed droopier than ever.

"Well, according to my watch," said Heather, "it took us thirty-four minutes to come down that river, so it will take us at least twice that long to get back. But probably more than that, the way you guys move."

I clenched my fists and pressed my lips together tightly. Heather always had to be right. I held my temper; she sure can get on anyone's nerves.

"Let's go! I can't wait to change out of these wet jeans. They're heavy. Ah-choo!" My body shook from the cold.

CHAPTER 11

DEAR DIARY,

Errors in judgment can be valuable. That is, if we learn from them. My Father is always telling me this. He says I am to learn from my mistakes. Canoeing on the river today was one of them. It took us more than two hours to get back to camp that afternoon.

I was really tired, especially from carrying the canoe. We took too many breaks.

We were lucky. Big B was nowhere around. In fact, no one was around. Everyone was at the chow hall. I skipped eating dinner. All I wanted to do was crawl into my bunk and die.

The only one who was hungry was Bambi. I don't think anything takes her appetite away.

I think I'm losing weight. My jeans are getting bigger. My face looks thinner. I may be skinny by the time camp ends.

Last night, around nine o'clock, Big B dropped in on us. "Well, Groundhogs, why weren't you at dinner tonight?" she asked in her booming voice. None of us said anything. Number one, we were already asleep. Number two, none of us are particularly fond of her. It's like she just waits for one of us to make a mistake.

I feel like I'm walking on eggs and if I step too hard, what a mess. I get goose bumps just thinking about it.

If I didn't know any better, I would've thought that Brenda was a sergeant in the army. Maybe, she's practicing for it.

Anyway, Big B was dying to know why we hadn't shown up for dinner.

She wasn't happy with any of us for not answering, and stomped out slamming the screen door behind her.

Nancy Ann thinks we should try to be nicer to her. Then, maybe, she would try to be nicer to us. Maybe, Nancy Ann is right. Daddy says that there are not enough nice people in this world and we all need to try harder to be one. Of course, he was referring to Mr. Evans, one of our neighbors, who always lets his dogs run all over the neighborhood to get their exercise and do their business. People were really upset and talking didn't do much good. The dogs still ran the streets and lawns. One day some of the neighbors got together and collected all the dog poop and put it on his front steps. Boy, was Mr. Evans mad, but after that the dogs stayed in their own yard. I think people can do better by talking. Maybe, we should try it Nancy Ann's way. I'm not sure what we can do to make peace though.

I'd better stop now. Inspection time is any minute. Our bungalow looks great! We even collected all the dust balls which were under the bunks. Wash time is after breakfast. We had piled our wet clothes from yesterday in the corner.

They smelled musty this morning. Lucky for us, Big B didn't see them last night.

I couldn't stand to get into trouble again.

Today Nancy Ann and I are going down to the stables with Heather as our guide.

I've never been horseback riding. This shouldn't be too traumatic, not like the exciting canoe ride we had.

CHAPTER 12

THERE HAS TO be an easier way to get up on a horse, I thought as I glanced up at the raggedy-looking saddle. It just seemed so far up there. And that thing that Heather had called a stirrup, how could I put my foot into that? Everything was starting off wrong. My confidence slowly dissolved. Sugarcake, that's my horse, must've been nervous. She kept moving in every direction. I turned to say something to Nancy Ann but held my tongue in time. Nancy Ann was already in her saddle.

Bambi stood at the corral gate and waved. She had decided not to put her life on the line today. After our canoe ride, I didn't blame her. It had been pretty nerve racking.

"Tracey, it's easy. Watch Heather! She showed me how."said Nancy Ann.

"Tracey, go over to the fence and climb up. Then you can get on. See?"

Heather got up so expertly. Why did Heather always have all the answers? I am waiting for the day she makes a mistake.

"There's nothing to riding a horse. I've spent

many Saturdays riding. My Uncle Stanley has a horse ranch."

Heather always ran off at the mouth when talking about herself, I thought. Now, she was the expert horsewoman.

"Pat Sugarcake as you get on her, Tracey," said Heather. "Let her know that you are attempting to communicate with her."

I didn't know that patting a horse meant communicating. Well, I learned something new again today. But why does it always have to be from Heather?

I never said I was athletic. But at that moment, I wished I were. Everyone was on their horse but me. Heather's horse, Spitz, was getting restless and whinnied. Sugarcake answered by taking a long step. I grabbed hold of her neck as I flung my right leg over the saddle.

"Hold on, Tracey," squeaked Nancy Ann, her voice breaking. I must have looked ridiculous. A horse's neck is quite large. My arms didn't fit.

"Now grab the reins and sit straight," said Heather. "You control your horse with the reins." I struggled to pull myself up from my slouched forward position.

"Let's go!" said Heather.

Heather was always in such a great hurry, I thought. Dad always said that it was better to take your time and do things right. I wondered if that included getting on a horse?

It was easy guiding Sugarfoot. She just followed the other horses. In fact, I didn't really have to put much effort into the whole business. My confidence grew as the horses wound their way through much-used pathways. Nothing could be nicer than the smell of pine trees. This was the best of Sugar Pine.

"Nancy Ann, does your fanny feel funny every time your horse takes a step?"

"Well, if you mean does my fanny go up and down every time, yes, it does. And when we're going downhill, I slide forward. I feel like I'm coming out of the saddle."

"Good, I'm glad I'm not alone."

"Look!" said Nancy Ann. "That bird!"

Over in the distance a large bird with a brilliant red head clung to a pine tree, pecking at it hard. The pecking sounded like a drummer beating on a hollow tree trunk.

"That's a Woodpecker," said Heather.

"But that big? That one is over a foot long," I said, hoping that Heather could be wrong.

"Woodpeckers can get very big. In fact, the deeper you go into the woods, the bigger and brighter they can become. "

She can be so annoying.

Nancy Ann looked at me and smiled meekly. "Can't win them all," she whispered.

"Yeah, but I wish I would win just one."

I kept stroking Sugarfoot as she walked

steadily on the path. I've heard of runaways. I figured if I kept communicating with her, everything would be kept under control.

"Over there!" Heather pointed to a pair of perfectly matched deer. In fact, they could have been a painting. Their markings were identical and so was their stance.

"Gosh, how utterly beautiful" breathed Nancy Ann.

I had to agree with her. I had never seen anything like that before.

"What do they eat?" I curiously asked Heather, who knew everything.

"About every kind of leaf you see around you, except pine needles and Oleander."

"I bet they don't eat poison oak," I said, sounding sure of myself.

Heather paused and said, "You're probably right, but I really don't know."

I couldn't believe that Heather didn't know something.

"I don't see any poison oak around, anyway," I stated matter-of-factly.

"Well if it's here, it blends in with everything else. It doesn't turn orangey-red till September. Anyway, I don't see any either."

Actually, I felt relieved when Heather said this. I get poison oak badly. One time, Dad was cleaning out an area down by the creek and later, much later, he gave me a hug. I was in the hospital emergency room that night. My arms had broken out in big red splotches. It's scary. People can die of it. I haven't met anyone who did, but they must have already died from it. It's so terrible.

"You know, we must've ridden for miles," I said. "Perhaps, we should turn around."

"This trail winds around the camp and back to the stables," said Heather.

"You're not tired, are you?"

"No, but I think my horse is."

"Horses can travel for hours and hours," said Heather, "but maybe you're right. I think we should hurry them along." Heather took her reins and slapped the side of her horse.

Now, I didn't mean for us to get into a full gallop, but Heather was off and going, and I couldn't protest after saying what I had.

"Tracey, I don't like going this fast, especially downhill," said Nancy Ann.

"Me either. Slow down Heather."

"Are you two chicken?"

"No, but I don't like galloping," I cried.

"You're not! You're only cantering."

Whatever you call it, my rear was feeling it. And my legs were wobbly. I felt like I had lost control, even though I'm sure I never had it in the first place.

Heather continued and of course, our horses followed. I kept patting Sugarfoot, hoping she and I were still communicating.

This sure didn't seem like communication to me.

Suddenly, Spitz reared up and landed hard. Yelping, Heather went up too and landed hard, not on her horse but on the ground via the bushes.

"Tracey," shrieked Nancy Ann. Spitz's reins had fallen to the ground. He took off down the trail leaving Heather sprawled unladylike in the middle of some bushes.

"Are you hurt?" I asked. I would have jumped off my horse like they do in the movies, but I knew I wouldn't have been able to get back on without a fence to help me. So neither Nancy Ann, or I budged from our saddles.

"You're lucky," said Nancy Ann, "you could've landed on some rocks. Those bushes broke your fall."

Heather didn't look like her usual self. And she didn't say very much.

"I'm not hurt. I'll have to ride back with one of you."

Nancy Ann helped pull her up to sit in front of her. Nancy Ann is nicer than I am.

Boy, Heather's fanny was going to feel those bruises for a few days. I could feel my own rear-end right now after all this riding.

Our ride was finished in silence. There wasn't much to say.

Just as we were coming up to the stables, Heather broke the silence.

"Listen guys, about my fall. You know something spooked my horse. That could happen to anyone. Do me a favor...don't tell anyone back at camp about it, okay?"

I smiled to myself. "Well, if it's not such a big thing, then you shouldn't mind."

"Especially, since you have been blowing your horn several days now about what a good horseperson you are," said Nancy Ann.

"But no sense telling anyone. I could've been hurt and I wouldn't want Brenda to tell Mrs. Scarfield."

"Well, maybe she's right, Tracey! It might cause a disturbance." Nancy Ann winked at me. Heather couldn't see it because she was sitting in front of her.

I was enjoying this. Heather is not one to ask anything of anyone. She wasn't that type. She was always in control.

"Well, let's think about it," I said. I thought I would just let her stew for a while.

I can really be mean if I want to be.

CHAPTER 13

DEAR SARAH,

It's easy to find the time to write today. My back muscles are still stiff, so I'm keeping a low profile. So is Nancy Ann. We must have ridden for miles on Monday. On a horse, of course. Galloping every minute. Well, maybe, not every minute.

That know-it-all Heather came too. Actually, she was our guide.

She's not as expert at riding horses as she thought. Something spooked her horse and Heather landed in the bushes. Everything would have been okay except those bushes were poison oak. Can you imagine? So Heather is in the infirmary right now. Yesterday, she looked awful! She woke up itching badly.

Tonight, we're having a camp cookout. The boys from Bigfoot are invited. It's really a camp social because there's dancing over on the tennis courts. They're going to turn on the outdoor lights. Music will be piped out over loudspeakers and everyone for miles will hear it. This time Daddy won't be around to tell them to turn it down. You know how he's always after me for my loud music.

Candy and Helen are on the social committee. Don't know how they got picked. They're anything but social. Unless, you call playing tennis ten hours a day, social. Don't know how they get away with it. Nancy Ann thinks their parents have an "in" with the Camp Director.

Anyway, the social committee is decorating the campgrounds.

Right now, they're pumping up balloons. In fact, our bungalow is filled with them. Bambi already popped two. Helen and Candy blew. It was so funny 'cause Bambi wasn't looking and she simply sat on them.

They volunteered Robin to help tie strings on them.

Robin is too nice. She can't say no. It was easy for me to say no.

Besides, my whole body is too sore even to tie silly knots in strings.

Hope it is fun tonight.

I still need to improve my tan. Nancy Ann and I plan to go swimming today after lunch. My bathing suit should look better on me now. I know I've lost weight.

Today's lunch menu is California Quiche. My poor taste buds. It's made of zucchini, yellow squash, and Swiss chard. Now you know why I'm losing weight.

I bet you're not having any problem eating with all that good food you're getting. Especially, hamburgers.

XOX Tracey

"Look out!" cried Helen.

A plastic garbage bag full of balloons had fallen down from a top bunk and had landed on top of me. Nancy Ann broke into laughter.

I attempted to ignore her and brushed the balloons away.

Bang! Pop!

"Tracey!" cried Candy.

"Be careful!" said Helen.

"You be careful! It's not my fault your balloons fell on me. I'm trying to write peacefully."

"Okay, you guys. Cut it out!" said Robin.

I felt myself turn red. Robin didn't usually speak up that way. For such a small size, she has quite an impact.

"Nancy Ann want to finish writing to Sarah? Then we can mail it tomorrow."

"Good idea. I owe her a letter."

"What's there to eat tonight?" T asked. "I hope not roasted tree bark dipped in honey sap. Ugh!"

"You're so cute, T. We're having hot dogs! What else would you have at a camp-out?" asked Candy curtly.

"Oh, my! Hot dogs!" said T. "Since when is that nutritious?"

"Since they make them with turkey. Where have you been?" said Helen.

"Yeah. Turkeys like you," T and her big mouth. I didn't mind it this time though.

"That's enough!" snapped Robin. Everyone looked at her in surprised silence. T pulled herself up from her squatting position and stomped out. Boy, Robin was beginning to get tough! No more shyness from her.

"Nancy Ann, we need to get going if we plan

on swimming. Let's go check out an inner tube. Are you finished yet?"

"Just a minute," Nancy Ann said.

I looked into the mirror. Only one pimple. Not bad. Maybe, this health food worked after all. One thing about Nancy Ann having a thousand freckles, it wasn't easy to see a pimple when it sprouted.

"Come on, let's go! Get the radio. It's hidden under Robin's sleeping bag." I grabbed my beach towel and covered up the radio. I didn't want to advertise Nancy Ann's radio to Big B. She had sneaked it in her sleeping bag. Smart!

CHAPTER 14

"OH, WHAT AM I going to do?" I wailed. "Careful, Nancy Ann, that hurts!"

"I told you to put some lotion on. I always wear it. I have to."

"Yeah, or you would be one big freckle and then you might peel off."

"Well, at least I have enough brains to put on sunscreen to keep from burning. Look at you. You're a mess."

She was right. I could see me at the dance tonight. Utterly miserable.

"Can I put anything on for after burn?"

"What happened to you?" asked Bambi as she came bursting in, the screen door slamming hard.

"Don't ask!" I said.

"Wow. You won't want anyone next to you tonight. Bet that hurts," said Robin standing behind Bambi.

"I think we should take your picture so you will remember this day," laughed T, pulling at a knuckle.

I didn't feel like remembering. This moment was painful enough.

"I bet Sarah would like a picture," said Nancy Ann smiling.

"You're all so funny. Ohhh...I think I'll take a cool shower. Maybe, that will help."

"I'll go too. I feel greasy. Then, I will need a hot shower and I can't."

"You're such a comic. Let's go. But not so fast. My legs hurt too. In fact, every part of me hurts."

"You're going to be sore tomorrow. It always hurts worse the next day."

"How would you know? Walk slower!"

"Well, look at the birds," said Helen from the tennis court. Candy and Helen were up on the ladder hanging balloons.

"And one of them has her red feathers on!" said Candy.

"Don't pay attention, Tracey. We have other things to do now like cooling off. Right?"

"My temperature goes up just being around those two."

"Never mind them. Let's concentrate on your burn."

"Careful, Nancy Ann. The straps are the worst...what can I wear tonight that won't hurt?"

"Hmmm...nothing that I can think of ... but you know Bambi has that wrap-around that she wears after swimming."

"That thing will go around me twice!" I shrieked.

"Can you think of something else?"

I grimaced as I pulled the rest of my bathing suit off. Nancy Ann can be so annoying. And so right. I didn't have much of a choice.

"I guess not." I carefully rinsed the soap off my back. Boy, tonight was going to be some social. I'll be the social wallflower with my skin being a bright cherry red.

Robin and Nancy Ann had draped the Hawaiian flower wrap loosely around me.

"I think it'll fall if I move," I said, trying to stand as straight as possible. I held my shoulders back as far as I could. Mother would have been proud of me. She was always after me for slumping over.

"You'll have to hold it up with your arms," sneered T. "I can see you dancing now. You'll look like a robot."

"Here's a sash to wrap around your top. That should help hold it up."

"I look so ridiculous! The red flowers not only show off my red skin but they make me look big."

"How can the flowers make you look big?" asked T. "That's only your imagination."

"Nancy Ann, is it my imagination or what?"

"Well... I..."

"I think we ought to go," said Robin. "We're all ready, right?"

"I'll go. But this is not one of my better nights," I said.

"Everyone's here except Heather," said T.

"Speaking of Heather, how is she T?" asked Nancy Ann.

"We stopped by to see her this afternoon. She's covered head to toe with cream. It kind of puts a damper on her vacation." said Robin.

"It's more like an itch," said T. Her knuckles cracked.

"Her face is all puffy. She must be really allergic to poison oak. She even has it in her ears. How she got it there, I don't know."

"It can go anywhere, believe me," I said. "I've had it pretty bad. If Heather didn't annoy me so much with her attitude, I would feel sorry for her. But, she's earned every itch."

"And just think, you and Heather have something in common," said T.

"I don't appreciate all your smart remarks."

"Okay, everyone. We don't have time for goofiness. Let's go. Those hot dogs, turkey or whatever, won't wait for us," said Robin.

"And the guys. They won't wait for us either," said T, tossing her long hair back with a flip of her head. T really had beautiful hair.

Shadows danced throughout the camp grounds. Moths flew in between the hanging lights which swayed as a breeze brushed against them.

"Boy, I don't mind that air," I said. "My skin really tingles."

"Speaking of tingles, Tracey. Look over there!"

Candy and Helen stood in the middle of the tennis courts surrounded by guys.

"Well, they sure headed down here fast," I said.

"Do you see what I see?" said Bambi, who didn't halt fast enough and crashed into the back of T as she stopped abruptly.

"Yep! I think we all do," groaned T.

"They think they're so good!" said Bambi, the corners of her eyes drooping. Her bottom lip poked out.

"Well, I don't know about you guys, but I'm hungry," said Robin.

"Me too," said Bambi, her spirits picking up.

"Go slower. Those hot dogs won't walk away," I said.

CHAPTER 15

I FINISHED UP two hot dogs, a dish of potato salad, and a soda. I looked over at Bambi gorging herself. My stomach muscles ached just watching her.

"Hey, Bambi, what number are you on?" I asked.

"Whaaat?" Bambi sputtered, pieces of food flying.

"How many hot dogs have you stuffed yourself with?" asked T.

"Well... I guess this is my third," said Bambi.

"No, that's your fifth," said Robin. "I know 'cause you had one of mine and you sneaked one in between."

Everybody laughed. I couldn't tell if Bambi was embarrassed or not, the glow of the fire made everyone's face red.

"Let's make s'mores," someone shouted.

"Where are the marshmallows?"

"What are s'mores?" asked Robin.

"Boy, you must have led a sheltered life!" said T.

"She has!" A masculine voice behind us all made us turn our heads. Two of the boys from Camp Bigfoot leaned against a tree.

"How long have you guys been standing there eavesdropping?" I asked indignantly.

"Well, you know we were invited here," said the boy in the yellow sweater.

"We were hoping more girls would be over at the tennis courts. It isn't so much fun dancing by ourselves," the other one said.

Everyone laughed including me. These boys weren't so bad.

"Let's roast these marshmallows first," said Bambi. "Want some?"

I suspected that Bambi would rather eat than dance anyway. I was relieved to keep my squatting position for a bit longer. The top of my wrap was inching its way downward.

"Hand me some graham crackers," said Nancy Ann.

"Here's the chocolate bars," said T.

"I like my marshmallow burned and real drippy," I said, licking my lips just thinking about it.

"Ugh, that's gross," said T.

"Gross, or not, that's the way I like them," I said defiantly.

"That's the way I like marshmallows, too! Burnt all the way through," said the boy in the yellow sweater, who introduced himself as Paul.

Two s'mores later, I felt sick. I knew I had gained several pounds, but I couldn't resist melted marshmallows, especially burnt ones.

"Well, let's all go dancing now," said Paul. "What does everyone say?"

"Why not," said T jumping in.

"This fire feels so good. I'm not sure I want to leave it." My arms were wrapped tightly around my top, holding it on. And being sunburned, my skin was already warm.

"Yeah, it's really nice by the fire," said Nancy Ann.

"Well, I'm going. Come on, Robin. Are you coming Bambi?" asked T.

Bambi had marshmallows and chocolate smeared across her chin. "No, I think I'll stay by the campfire too."

"You just want another s'more," said T.

T was right. No sooner had they left than Bambi had another. This time with two chocolate squares.

"Nancy Ann, this fire is making me very warm. In fact, I'm hot."

"That's your sunburn talking. You need to cool off. Let's take a walk over by the tennis courts. We don't have to dance. Just watch."

"Okay, but help me up. I'm afraid if I move, this thing will fall off. Careful! Try helping without grabbing," I said wincing as Nancy Ann touched my arm.

"Well, here are the late birds!" shouted Helen.

"And here I thought they were a couple of chickens," said Candy tartly.

"I wonder if they can ever say anything nice," I muttered.

A few couples were dancing on the tennis courts. But there were more kids standing around outside of the courts. I knew there wasn't much to dancing, but I didn't know any steps.

And as if Nancy Ann was reading my mind, she said, "You know, Tracey, in the fall we can sign up for the ballroom dancing class after school."

"Maybe, if I manage my time better this year." I wasn't very good at planning things. Dad said it was another one of my lack of responsibilities. Oh well, maybe one day. I wondered if he would rather have a daughter like Heather. Hmm... probably not. Dad needed someone to train and retrain.

"Hi, Red. See you guys finally made it." It was Charlie, Paul's friend.

"Yeah... we just wanted our food to settle before we went dancing," said Nancy Ann.

"Ohhh... did you get burned," said another voice.

I turned around to face Paul. I backed up and bumped into Nancy Ann. I started to walk away, but Nancy Ann had grabbed the back of my wrap-around. It didn't look like I was going anywhere.

"Yeah, well I rubbed shoulders with Mr. Sun today," I said hesitantly.

"I couldn't tell till now. Back at the campfire everyone looked red. It must hurt! I guess you can't rub shoulders with me then."

"Well... anyway, I'm not into dancing tonight," I said. I was really uncomfortable. I knew Bambi's wrap was going to drop at any moment.

Within minutes, other boys had come over. Probably out of curiosity. Soon we had quite a gathering.

"Well, what do we have here?" said Candy.

"It looks like a group of turkeys with a red rooster in the middle," said Helen.

"Well, I believe someone is green with envy," whispered Nancy Ann. The music stopped just as Nancy Ann opened her mouth.

"I heard that! And I am not!" snapped Helen. The music blared nine notes out of the speaker hanging on a branch above our heads.

"Say, Red, would you like to walk to the lake?" said Charlie to Nancy Ann. "It's too noisy to talk around here."

"What do you think, Tracey? How are you feeling now?"

I took a side glance at Paul. He was taller than me by about three inches. His curly blonde hair hung down in his face. Paul was nice to look at. I wondered what Butch was doing right now. He was also nice to look at.

"Would you believe I'm freezing inside and my skin is hot outside?"

"Well, then you have to get your body to a happy balance," said Paul, flashing a smile.

I felt my face turn red. How could I not accept? Besides, the four of us would be together. It might be fun. I've not been one to like most boys. Boys were always so goofy. But my friend back home, Butch, was different. We had been friends since I was little. His family moved into our area when I was three. We had kissed once in front of the mailman. Butch wanted to show Mr. Jenkins that I was his girlfriend. It was one of those experiences that a girl never forgets. It was my first kiss. In fact, it was my only kiss. I was five.

The walk down to the lake was not bad. There was still most of a full moon to help show us the way.

I wasn't sure if my insides were nervous from being with my new friend or wondering if the Hawaiian wrap-around was going to let me down. Really down.

I found that if I sucked in my breath and made my lungs bigger, my top would stay up without my arms hugging me. Do you know how difficult it is to talk to someone with your lungs ballooned up? Let alone walk. Life can be very complicated.

Nancy Ann and Charlie talked continuously. They said enough for all of us. I felt sorry for Paul. I couldn't tell him how miserable I was. In fact, I didn't tell him much of anything. He must have thought I was a real drip.

"Watch your step," said Paul as I stumbled slightly.

Never again will I sunbathe without sunscreen, I thought.

"I think the animals are out tonight!" said Charlie who was up ahead of us leading the way.

A rustle in the underbrush got my attention immediately. A shiver went up my backbone.

"What was that?" asked Nancy Ann.

"Probably just a night animal stepping on some dry leaves," said Paul.

I wondered how old Paul was. He seemed to be older than the other boys I had seen at the camp social, and he was definitely older than Butch.

"Well, I wish that night animal would go away," said Nancy Ann trying to whisper but not succeeding.

We had stopped walking. But the rustling hadn't. We were only a few yards from the lake and the water lapped up against the shore. The rustling continued as we headed down towards the water.

I pictured a creature, half reptile, half mammal, with long sharp teeth crawling on its belly.

"Tracey, remember that story about the lake monster?"

I didn't answer. It was a story I remembered very well.

"What lake monster?" asked Paul.

"The one..." My words were cut off by a huge splash of water.

The lake monster was gone. Or whatever it had been. We decided not to wait around and headed back to the camp.

CHAPTER 16

July 18

DEAR DIARY,

Getting up early isn't so bad. I guess I'm getting used to it. For some reason, I woke up before the bugle went off this morning. I even have a few free minutes before we eat.

My favorite meal here is breakfast. It's the safest. I can depend on what we're going to have. I chose eggs – no matter how they cooked them. Also, bran muffins. Especially, with dates in them not raisins. Raisins make me go to the bathroom. So does bran, but I don't need a double dosage.

Everything is really neat. I mean really neat. I met a nice guy. He's not like Butch 'cause he's older. In fact, he's a lot older. I found out that he's almost fourteen. Would Dad raise an eye brow.

Today we're playing a softball game against the Camp Bigfoot guys. I'm glad I brought my best Nikes. The striped ones which match my favorite jeans.

My sunburn is better today. I sure was hot & cold last night... all at the same time. It was sort of like having the flu without a temperature and a runny nose. I even had to wear Bambi's Hawaiian wrap-around because everything else was too close to my sunburn. I looked awful. I didn't think anyone would even take a look at me. Was Candy and Helen ever jealous when Nancy Ann and I met Paul and Charlie. Or rather when they met us.

When Candy and Helen came in last night, they made all kinds noises and even turned on the lights.

Big B had barged in so fast the entire bungalow shook. She jumped on Candy and Helen for making such a ruckus. I think she thought Nancy Ann and I had turned on the lights. She sure got a big surprise. It was funny seeing her face. Then Big B jumped on Bambi because she started laughing.

We all joined in. After all, she couldn't put us all on restriction.

The worse thing that happened was to Bambi. She must have drunk too much soda with her s'mores. She laughed so hard that she peed. She just sat there on the bunk laughing and peeing at the same time. Can you imagine? I would have died if that had been me.

I think I'll skip lunch today. I ate so much last night that Bambi's Hawaiian wrap-around may fit pretty soon. I can run better on an empty stomach, anyway.

I want to look good on the softball field when we play our game today.

I'm finishing my entry during breakfast – we're having under-water eggs this morning. I mean poached. And Florida-grown orange juice. So says the cook.

That smudge on the bottom of the page is honey from my bran muffin. Hope it doesn't make the pages stick together.

"Everyone ready? Let's go." said Nancy Ann getting up from the table.

It was a good thing I brought my mitt along. And my A's cap.

"Bungalows 13, 14, and 16 report to the

softball field in five minutes," a loud speaker boomed out over the chow hall. Big B didn't really need the loud speaker with her voice.

"Tracey, do you think we stand a chance?" said Nancy Ann peeking over my shoulder at my diary.

"Come on, we'd better get out there and warm up," said T, pulling on her fingers. "It's been a while since I played."

"Yeah, we have to give them our best shot," murmured Robin. I didn't think Robin was into sports. But since her shyness left, nothing about her surprised me.

"Does anyone have an extra mitt for me to use?" asked Robin.

We all looked at each other. "No," I said, "but if you ask one of the guys, I bet they would let you borrow one of theirs."

"Yeah, that would be a good way to meet them," said Nancy Ann smiling.

Dear Diary,

I'm sort of continuing where I left off this morning. It's after our game. The guys were more than fair. Nancy Ann was up first. She swung too low; then too high; then she struck out.

I was up after Nancy Ann. Believe it or not, I hit the ball on my first try. And I got to second, but only because Big B, who was the first base coach, made me run. I always get nervous running more bases than one.

T got me in by hitting a triple. She's pretty good.

Well, my gut feeling was right. Tiny Robin is full of surprises. She hit a grounder and it went through Charlie's legs. Boy, was he embarrassed. Anyway, Robin came home. She was so happy. So were we because we were ahead three to nothing.

Oh, I forgot to tell you that the boys gave us five outs to their three; that helped a little.

Their first batter up would be what my Dad would call professional. He was good. I was pretty impressed by the way the batter took his stance. But, then the guy hit a strike.

The next hit was a high fly and guess where it went? Right towards me. I knew I was going to miss it 'cause I couldn't help closing my eyes as it came toward me. Nancy Ann told me later that it came within inches of me and then bounced high into the outfield area near T. Didn't do much good. The guy was fast and he came home.

Big B really got into the game and kept yelling at us to hustle.

Bambi's job was to sit on the sideline and encourage us. Actually, there was a pretty good audience. It makes you try harder when people are watching.

Especially, if they're boys. I had a feeling that Paul was watching every move I made.

I tried to sneak a look at him. But I couldn't without him looking at me. I could feel my face turn warm.

I guess I did hit the ball better 'cause Paul told me to step into the pitch with my right foot. He said it to me quietly as he passed me on the field. He didn't want the other guys to hear.

Diane, one of our teammates, got hurt. Nothing bad. She twisted her right wrist as she hit a foul ball. So, she used her left arm. The only problem was that she got confused. After she hit the ball, she ran to third. Everyone screamed, but she didn't realize her mistake until she ran into Robin coming into third. It was the craziest thing I've ever seen.

After the game, we headed down to the canteen. Paul wanted to buy me a soda. I wonder if this means he likes me. I got a Diet Coke. Do you think he will think I feel that I'm overweight now?

Charlie is really funny. He sure gets Nancy Ann to talk. She can say some of the dumbest things when she talks too much. I heard her ask Charlie about his family. He has lots of brothers and sisters. She asked him why were there so many kids.

Charlie just stuttered a bit and said something about his Mom and Dad liking each other a lot. I pretended I didn't hear. I have better things to talk about.

Got to go. Will write later.

Oh yeah, the boys won the game. It was a pretty good game, too. The score was sixteen to ten. Big B said we did a good job at representing our camp. She never says anything nice to us. So, this was a big deal. Dad would have called this progress.

CHAPTER 17

THEY WERE CHEWY, crunchy, crispy, and not nutritious; I thought as I smacked my lips together.

"These are the best chocolate chip cookies," I said gratefully relishing every bit.

"That's the good thing about being sick," said Heather munching on a cookie.

"Mother came down yesterday afternoon. She wanted me to come home, but we have another seven days and there's still so many things to do." Heather actually sounded happy to be back with us.

She seemed a lot nicer. The poison oak must've done something to her head. She should get sick more often. I looked at Nancy Ann who was more involved in the cookies than the conversation.

"Well, these sure are great!" said Robin.

"Yep! A nice way to celebrate your coming back to bungalow fourteen," muttered Bambi between bites.

"Well, did anything exciting happen during my absence?" asked Heather.

"Not too much," said Nancy Ann. Humph, not too much I thought. I've just met the cutest boy I've ever known. And Nancy Ann didn't do so badly herself.

The box of cookies was almost gone. Two cookies and a box of crumbs was all that was left.

I wondered who was going to get the last two.

A knock on the door answered my thoughts. Of course, Big B didn't wait for us to invite her in.

"Health food cookies? Were these left for me?" said Big B looking at the two cookies greedily.

"Er....ah...why not? We've all had our fill... right?" said Heather. She gave us a meek smile and gave up her last two cookies. They would've been hard to divide anyway among the six of us.

"What's on the agenda for tomorrow?" Asked T.

"Tomorrow night is the camp talent show. Have you forgotten? It was announced last Monday."

"Jeepers! I'd forgotten," said Robin.

"Me, too! Do we have to?" moaned T.

I didn't have any talent to show off.

"Well, it's volunteer," said Big B, "but there's a prize for the most unusual act."

"Yeah, I can see you girls falling on your faces," laughed Helen. Candy joined in, "No one has any talent around here."

"Well, wait 'til you see our act!" said Nancy Ann protesting.

Those rats, I thought.

"Yeah, Nancy Ann and I had been working on our act for this past week."

"Really? And where have you been practicing?" asked Candy.

"Well, I'll let you girls get your act together. It's everybody for themselves. It's a contest." And with that, Big B headed out the bungalow, the screen door slamming behind her, the second cookie in her hand.

I thought of the back screen of our house. Mother was constantly yelling at me for letting it slam. She kept hoping I would grow out of it. She wouldn't be happy knowing my camp counselor slammed the screen door too.

"Well, we'd all better come up with something good for tomorrow," said T flatly.

"Let's sleep on it. I'm tired. I'm still itching. That medicine makes me sleepy," yawned Heather.

"I'm going to bed," grumbled Bambi as she climbed uncertainly up the ladder. Robin eyed Bambi carefully 'til she reached the top bunk. She then crawled onto her bed.

"I'm taking a shower. Nancy Ann, are you coming?"

I grabbed my towel and soap.

But, no sooner had the screen door slammed

than Nancy burst out, "Tracey, what are we going to do? We have no act."

"Maybe... a stand-up comedian? We're funny, but not that funny."

"When was the last time you carried a tune?"

"In the shower but then Dad told me to close the window so that the neighbors wouldn't hear."

" I don't think I'm that good. Anyway, I want to do something different," I said.

"We're going to have to come up with something really good. Does any talent run in your family, Tracey?"

"Not really... I do have one cousin who is a dancer. He's really good on his feet."

"Does that give you any ideas for us?"

"Maybe, if Johnathan were here, he could help us."

"Johnathan?"

"Yes. Johnathan Franklin McLaren. That's my cousin."

"You never talk about him," stated Nancy Ann.

"There's not much to talk about. We're really not close. We only see him on special occasions. He's a super guy."

"Special occasions?"

"Yeah, like when my Aunt and Johnathan come to visit. Maybe, once or twice a year."

"Well, that doesn't help us now and besides,

he is not here." huffed Nancy Ann as she finished drying her hair.

On our way back to the bungalow, Nancy Ann yelped, "I've got an idea!"

"Yeah?"

"We can do mime dancing. You know, while mimicking someone else."

I looked at her. She can really be deep at times. "What do you have in mind?" I asked.

"Well, tomorrow we should look for some music."

"Okay, let's do our star search research tomorrow. My brains are on disaster mode right now."

When I'm tired, I'm quiet. I just don't have the energy to think, let alone talk. That's the thing about close friends, they learn to know you. All the way back to our bungalow, Nancy Ann and I were quiet. Very quiet.

CHAPTER 18

HOURS LATER, NANCY Ann and I found ourselves sitting frustrated on a fallen tree. We had left the girl's camp earlier, hoping to find a private place where we could practice. So far, we had practiced nothing.

"Tracey, what are we going to do? And after we told Candy and Helen, we had been practicing on it all week."

I had no answer. I was feeling pretty bad. I sat squatted with my head buried in my hands. A noise behind me made me look up.

Pine needles fell all over me.

"What the..."

Hey, what's this?" yelled Nancy Ann.

"What do we have here?" said Paul. "Two lost little Red Riding Hoods?"

"Yeah, and I suppose you are the big bad wolves," sneered Nancy Ann.

"Wolves maybe, but not bad."

Each time I saw Paul with his blond hair falling in his face, my stomach jumped a little. Dad would have called it a case of nerves.

"What are you doing here?" repeated Paul.

"Nothing much," I said. "We're supposed to be getting our act together for tonight's talent show, but we're fizzled out just thinking."

"Oh, that's what I smell burning. You both need new batteries," laughed Charlie.

"How can you make jokes at a time like this?" said Nancy Ann pleadingly.

"Can't you see we have a challenge."

"Problems are made to be solved," said Paul.

I couldn't say a thing. Even with my jumping stomach, I was too depressed.

"Well, what kinds of ideas have you come with?" asked Paul.

"The thing we want to do the most is a soft shoe mime act. But we need background music..." said Nancy Ann. "Say, you guys wouldn't have any music we could use?"

"At our clubhouse we have all kinds of music. Want to go check it out?" said Paul.

"You know, your camp is off-limits to us," I said.

"Besides, I have a better idea!" said Charlie smiling. "I believe you girls have come to the right place. It just so happens that I have brought my violin with me."

"Violin!" both Nancy Ann and I chimed together.

I wasn't particularly fond of the violin. I had never seen one in any rock group. And I couldn't imagine one in our act. How would the camp like it? How would I like it? Violins reminded me of orchestras, not mime acts.

"This is a very special violin. It's electric."

"I've never heard of an electric violin," said Nancy Ann excitedly.

I couldn't imagine it sounding any better than a real one just because you plugged it in.

"Well, I do believe we had better get a move on if we are to put your act together," said Paul.

He held his hand out to help me up.

"Where are we going?" I asked.

"To Camp Bigfoot."

"Tracey, we've gotten into enough trouble. This time we'd better get permission from Big B."

"You're right. Can you guys wait here? We'll be back."

It took us a good half hour to find Big B. Getting her okay wasn't easy.

"Practice in the boys' camp? Can't you practice here?" Big B bellowed when she was upset.

"Then everyone will know what we're doing. We need electricity and we want everyone to be surprised."

"Humph! You two have put me through a lot this summer. You can sure stretch the camp rules."

"Please, just this once. We're asking for one favor," I asked. Nancy Ann and I exchanged looks.

Behind me my fingers were crossed. Big B loved to lecture.

"Well, be back here before the chow bell rings," Big B said gruffly.

"Oh, one more thing," I said meekly.

"One more thing! You asked for one favor!" shouted Big B.

"Charlie has to be in the act. His violin will be our background music," I said.

"Maybe you could record it." Big B had all the answers.

"It won't be as effective... and besides, we're short on time," whined Nancy Ann.

"Gosh, what am I going to do with you two? Go on; get out of here."

Nancy Ann and I tore out of the camp grounds fast. We were afraid Big B might think of something to change her mind.

"I bet she hated to be so nice," said Nancy Ann.

"Maybe, she likes to sound hard but she's really soft underneath. I think she's a lot nicer than she puts on. I hope it's not my imagination."

"Tracey, I'm not sure I like practicing with Charlie and Paul watching."

"Yeah, I was thinking about that myself. Just being around Paul is bad enough. The guys watching us perform are not going to make it any easier."

"Well, Charlie is going to have to be there with his violin."

"Over here..." Charlie and Paul were waiting behind some bushes.

On the way to the boy's camp, we told the guys about our cabin mates and some of the experiences we had all shared together. We ended up talking about know-it-all Heather. We never talked about Candy or Helen since we never included them or were included with them in any activity.

"Is Heather always that way?" asked Paul.

"Yes," we both said.

"It doesn't always make it easy living together under the same roof, does it?" asked Charlie.

"What's Heather going to do for the show?" asked Paul.

"We aren't sure. She's been pretty secretive about the whole thing. Her mother is bringing her costume up to camp. Heather undoubtedly has something up her sleeve," I said, thinking she would probably win.

Paul looked at Charlie. "Well, let's get going, you two have a lot of work ahead of you. Let's get my violin and get started," said Charlie.

We couldn't believe the music. Charlie was really good. He hooked his violin up to an amp. The best music poured out. Nancy Ann and I listened for more than an hour before we started on our act.

It was as hot as any rock music could ever be. Before we started practicing, Nancy Ann asked Charlie if we could practice in a room where no one could watch us. By four, we had it together, or at least that's what Charlie and Paul told us.

"Do you think we have a chance?" asked Nancy Ann.

"Well, we haven't seen the other acts, but as far as entertainment, you two are really good. Now, how about costumes?" asked Paul.

"Ohhh, Tracey, we forgot about that."

"How about using colors that look good under a black light?" said Paul. "We can get a black light from the camp office."

An hour later, we not only had the light, the costumes, but also the face make-up.

We were going to be terrific.

We left Camp Bigfoot on top of the world. Charlie and Paul helped us carry our outfits back.

"We'll meet you back here at seven-thirty," said Paul, as we loitered on the outskirts of Camp Sugar Pine near the canteen.

"Good, that will give us plenty of time to eat and dress," said Nancy Ann.

"Eat! You're eating! I'm not! I'm too... too nervous," I said.

"You look great!" said Robin. "What neat outfits."

"We do look good, don't we!" I said as I tucked my black shirt into my black pants. I rubbed the last bit of crème off of my fingers and put on the white gloves.

"Thanks," said Nancy Ann. "My face sure feels greasy and heavy with all this stuff on."

"Boy, I never want to get into make-up," murmured Robin as she helped T by drawing freckles on her face.

"I'm glad I'm going to be in the audience," Bambi said, as she buttoned T's dress up the back.

"What song are you going to sing?" I asked.

"That's a surprise. Just wait," said T.

"Everyone's so secretive," said Heather as she pulled on her bright silver tights. "Mother did a wonderful job of picking out my costume."

"Yeah, some people have it pretty easy," said T.

"You do look gorgeous," sighed Robin.

I had to admit that Heather did look good. Oh well, it was her act that counted.

"Tracey, it's seven-twenty. We have to go."

"Okay." I took a last-minute glance in the mirror, nodded with satisfaction and turned to face Nancy Ann. Except for her bright red hair, we could have been twins. Our faces were white masks, with penciled on eye lashes and bright red mouths and cheeks.

Nancy Ann looked at me, looked at the mirror and broke into laughter.

"Don't laugh, you two. You'll mess up your make-up."

Robin was right. Boy, make-up was too much trouble. If growing up meant you had to wear make-up, then becoming an adult was going to be a lot of work.

CHAPTER 19

"**CHARLIE, YOU LOOK** great!" said Nancy Ann excitedly.

"I have to admit you do look good. I wouldn't have recognized you." laughed Paul. "You three could pass for anyone in your mime costumes. I especially like your coat tails." Paul pointed to the pieces of cloth Robin had sewn onto a navy jacket of Charlie's.

Charlie blushed. "Bear in mind, I've never worn so much make-up. The closest I've ever come to this stuff was for a Halloween party when I went as Bozo the Clown. I didn't like it then."

"Me either," I said. My face felt stiff. But the mirror that Paul held up for me, told me I looked pretty good.

"How's your stomach, Nancy Ann?"

"Well, I could use another one at the moment."

"I want to watch out front so I think I'd better get myself situated."

"Don't let the other girls see you! Remember, you guys aren't supposed to be over here. Big B gave us permission for Charlie and you weren't included. Don't mess us up."

Waiting backstage made my stomach worse. Big B was doing her introductory speech. Her words could barely be heard above the screaming of the excited audience.

I pulled the curtains apart and peeked out. Everyone in camp was here!

"Nancy Ann, this is not going to be easy."

"Yeah, my feet can't even hold me up, let alone do our number."

"Take some deep breaths. That should help!"

"There's Bambi and Robin," squeaked Nancy Ann.

"Help me with these tights. They're slipping," complained Charlie.

"I don't see Paul. I wonder where he went to," I said still looking at the crowd. I hoped he wouldn't miss our performance.

The first number went on. One of the girls from bungalow twelve was doing a juggling act. Her two oranges went to three. Someone threw in an apple. And that was her downfall. The apple was the first to drop and then the oranges.

"Where's Heather? She goes on before we do."

"Maybe she chickened out," said Nancy Ann.

"Not her. She's too confident. Heather wouldn't miss this for the world," I said.

"Charlie, are you okay?" asked Nancy Ann.

"Not really. I don't see why I couldn't have dressed like myself!"

"You know why. Big B said you had to disguise yourself if you were going to be in our act. No boys, remember?" Nancy Ann sounded exasperated.

"Yeah, I remember. I shouldn't have volunteered my talents. I didn't think I'd have to dress up as a mime too. Hey, she's pretty good." One of the girls was mouthing the words to a record sung by Bruno Mars and Ed Sheeran. Half of her face was made-up as Bruno Mars and the other side was Ed Sheeran. In fact, her costume was cut in half too. Her wig was straight on one side, and curly on the other. Every time she sang one or the other person, her voice changed.

Both Nancy Ann and I stood with our mouths open. Charlie was right. Her act was really good. It was fun watching her.

"We aren't that good," whispered Nancy Ann.

"Maybe not, but we'll try."

"Well, I'm good and you're with me," said Charlie.

Big B rushed up to us, almost knocking us over. "Where's Heather? She's on next!"

"We don't know." I looked around backstage. Bright, colorful costumes flashed in front of us, but no Heather.

"Maybe she's a no-show," said Charlie.

"That's not like her," I said. "She would never back out. Besides, she thinks she's the best and wants to show everyone."

Big B was not happy. Every time she got her feathers ruffled her body ballooned up and she became twice her size.

"Well, we can't wait for her. Who's on next?"

"I am," said a little girl with an even littler voice.

"What's she going to do?" whispered Charlie.

Before Nancy Ann or I could answer, she walked out onto the stage and sat down at the piano.

One of my mother's favorite musical pieces came tumbling out. Bach or Beethoven. I never could keep them straight.

"That piano needs tuning," said Charlie.

I couldn't tell. It sounded pretty good to me.

Two more acts to go. I gulped.

The tallest and skinniest girl in camp waddled out onto the stage wearing a big yellow chicken costume. 'Old MacDonald Had a Farm' came out of her mouth. It was the funniest thing I had ever seen, let alone heard.

Then the moment I had been waiting for... Candy and Helen. They had been so secretive... so boastful.

My mouth dropped open.

"I don't believe it!" said Nancy Ann, hitting a note higher than normal, even for her.

Candy was dressed up as "Big B." She had on an extra, extra large size uniform with Brenda's name sewn on the pocket. Her uniform must have been stuffed with all kinds of junk. She had bulges coming out everywhere. Somewhere, she had got a short, straight wig. And her face was blushed with red.

"Who's Helen?"

Helen had spectacles propped up on her nose. She wore Bermuda shorts and had brushed on splotches of red on her knees. "She must be Mrs. Scarfield," squealed Nancy Ann.

The crowd went wild.

I looked over at Big B. She had disappeared. I looked for Paul. He was nowhere in sight. He was doing a good job of getting lost.

It was kind of embarrassing watching the girls. They did a soft shoe act to some rinky dink music. Every time Candy did a shuffle her uniform bobbled in one or in another direction.

"I'm sure glad I'm not in their shoes. Mrs. Scarfield won't be too happy over this," I said.

"Well, don't worry about it, Tracey, we have our own act to think about."

All too soon Big B appeared and pulled the curtains apart for us.

The next few minutes were crazy. If I were to sit down and tell anyone everything Nancy Ann and I did or didn't do, I couldn't. I was a bundle of nerves. Charlie's music made our act look very good. Nancy Ann and I just fell into step with it. Our bodies withered and waved, gyrated and pranced; it was fun being hidden behind the heavy make-up and doing things you wouldn't normally do. And it was easy to move to Charlie's music. The three minutes on stage seemed long. Then the audience yelled and clapped. We were a hit!

"Boy! I'm glad that's over!" exclaimed Nancy Ann.

"Me too; my armpits are drenched."

"You two girls were really good!" Charlie's voice sounded a little surprised.

"I'm glad you were with us," laughed Nancy Ann.

"I wonder where Paul is?" I couldn't see him anywhere.

"There's nowhere else to look!" said T speaking about Heather.

"She couldn't just disappear off the face of the earth!" said Robin.

"Maybe, we should send out a search party for her," I said smiling.

"This is serious," said Robin. "She's a missing person."

"You're right. Let's organize a search party," I said. There were always so many stories in the news about missing kids. It was frightening.

I pulled on my hoodie.

"Hey everyone! Heather's been found!"

"Where?"

"Where is she?'

"Who found her?"

"I don't know. She's coming now."

Nancy Ann opened the screen door.

"Heather!" What happened?"

"Where were you?"

"Did you chicken out?"

Heather looked pale and her once-pretty costume looked rumpled. I had never seen her look so bad.

"On my way over to the talent show I was jumped. Someone put a nasty potato sack over my head and then kidnapped me."

"Kidnapped you!" said Nancy Ann and I together.

"Who would do that?" I asked. "They didn't take you very far."

"You think I'm making it up?" Heather glared. "Why would I?"

"You didn't want to perform. That's all!"

"You chickened out!" laughed T.

"I did not! I'm not lying! I was kidnapped!"

"Well, I guess we'll have to believe you, since we can hear only your side of the story," I said. Everyone snickered.

"You're all so awful."

"Maybe, it was the lake monster. I hear he's on the rampage again," said T.

Everyone roared with laughter.

Heather glared at us and stomped out of the bungalow to the showers with her towel.

"Hey, what's going on here?" yelled Big B as she came thundering through the screen door.

"Didn't you see Heather," asked T. "She claims someone kidnapped her!"

Everyone snickered.

"Can you believe that she'd think we'd fall for that!" said Nancy Ann.

"Humph! This bungalow is always doing something to keep things going. I'm not sure I can believe any of you. I've more important things to do than hang around here listening to stories." And Big B marched out huffing.

I looked at the others. Camp life was sure exciting. But after all, my life was never dull.

CHAPTER 20

July 21

DEAR SARAH,

So many things have happened since my last letter. I can't think of which one to write about — I guess the camp talent show.

I know I'll probably leave out a lot of crazy things but they are all in my diary. You can read about them later.

Have you ever seen a mime? I was one for our camp talent show. And so was Nancy Ann. Boy, were we painted! Our make-up must have been an inch thick. It took us two bath towels to scrape it off.

But it was worth it. We tied for first place.

The whole thing was very exciting, but was I nervous. Yes, imagine me being nervous!

Nancy Ann couldn't stand still while we waited to go on stage.

The only thing that calmed us was our friend, Charlie. Actually, he's mostly Nancy Ann's friend. He played the electric violin. I think the music helped soothe our nerves.

In our costume we were really disguised. We even had gloves on. No one could tell who we were. I asked Big B not to announce our names 'til later – so we used our stage names, 'The Silent Duo Plus One'.

We didn't want anyone to know in case we messed up, but I didn't tell Big B that. We told her that it would take the fun out of our mime act since we were already hidden behind all that make-up.

Anyway, we weren't a bomb but a hit.

Speaking of bombs, I think the biggest explosion happened after the show was over; and Heather turned up. She didn't make the show. She said someone had kidnapped her, but of course no one believed her. It was a ridiculous story. Heather said that someone tied her up in a potato sack and left her till after the show.

Then somehow, the bag became untied and she found her way back to camp. Can you imagine a story like that!

Oh, I forgot to tell you our prize. Gift coupons to go into town and treat ourselves to a vegetarian pizza at Mountain Pete's. Isn't that crazy? Even the camp tells us what to order at a restaurant.

Speaking of last minutes, we have only a few more days here. Can't wait to see you. There's so much to tell. You'll be home in the middle of August, right?

I expect to find a pile of postcards and letters from you. I didn't want Mother to forward any of your mail. It might get lost.

Don't laugh! Once Nancy Ann sent me a letter when she went with her family on a vacation. She had sent me some flowers she had pressed.

Someone else must have got them because I never did. So now, I'm more careful. Besides, I know it takes a while for mail to come from New York. I know it has more of a chance of getting lost.

Give my love to everyone – especially Nikko. Is he still shedding?

XOX Tracey

Sarah, just a hi from me. I'll write you when I get home. I've run out of my Panda note paper.

Love,
Nancy Ann

CHAPTER 21

"TRACEY!" THE SCREEN door slammed hard, I jumped and jerked my head around. I now knew how my mother felt when I slammed the backscreen door. Boy, was Mother going to see a changed me.

"Tracey! Nancy Ann! Let's go swimming! Everyone's going down to the hole," said Robin.

Robin had slowly come out of her cocoon over the past few weeks and now she was a regular little go-getter.

"Come on. Get ready, Bambi. You're going too," she said.

"Me?"

"Yeah. Ask Big B if you can use her life jacket. She won't mind. After all, she doesn't want to see you drown."

"Yeah, it's better to be a lot wet than a little drowned," said T.

"You're too funny," sighed Nancy Ann sounding bored.

"Why not! I could use a good swim," I said looking at my finished letter. I folded Sarah's letter into three parts and stuffed it into an envelope, licking it closed.

"Here, put this poppy inside," said Nancy Ann as she undid the wet flap. Nancy Ann and her pressed flowers. She was too much. Each of Sarah's letters had a different kind of flower inside.

"Hey, you're not supposed to pick poppies!" said Robin.

"Robin's right," smirked Heather. "That could cost you a big fine."

"Fine?"

"Yes, as in money. If you're caught picking California poppies, you'll have to pay five hundred dollars."

"Or maybe, go to jail," said Robin.

"Jail?" Nancy Ann's face was one big freckle. She looked nervous.

"Yes, as in prison."

"Tracey!" Nancy Ann's voice hit a very high note.

"Don't listen to them. No one saw you and no one knows but us. And no one is going to say anything."

"Well, I suggest you don't do it again, Nancy Ann," said Heather with a huff.

I pretended not to hear Heather's remark and reached for my swim suit.

"Let's go. All this talk over a little flower."

"It's not just a flower. It's our state flower!" said Heather.

I winced. Heather always had to have the last word. I sure won't miss her when camp was over.

T cracked her knuckles one by one.

"Must you do that!" said Heather. "That's so unlady like."

"I must!" And T slammed out of the door, throwing her towel over her shoulder.

Bambi pulled her hoodie over her head and smiled. "I'm ready," she said.

"Well, I guess we all are. Heather, are you coming too?"

"Is that an invitation or are you hoping I would say no?" asked Heather.

"Whatever you like," said Robin without hesitating.

I frowned as I heard the screen door slam behind me. I sure wasn't going to miss that either. Maybe. I would ask Dad to take our screen door off at home. It didn't make much sense to keep it anyway. There wasn't one on the front of the house. So, the flies still got in.

"We'll be there in a few minutes. T, I want to mail Sarah's letter."

"And I need to get Big B's life jacket," said Bambi.

"Okay, come on, Robin, let's find a sunny spot on the rocks."

T's idea of rocks were large boulders. One was big enough to spread my towel out flat.

Nancy Ann found a spot on a boulder next to mine but down closer to the water.

I yawned. The sun made me sleepy. I took a deep breath. I could smell the water, the leaves of the tree branches hanging close to us, and something else. Probably flowers, since wild flowers were everywhere. I wondered if poison oak had a smell, and if it did, I hoped that smell wasn't one of them.

"Boy, this is the life. Those rays are saturating."

"Yeah, saturating," I smiled. Summer camp was coming to an end and all too quickly. I couldn't imagine myself getting into a routine at home again. Mother likes schedules. She would love to see me more organized. Especially, in my room.

Maybe, Camp Sugar Pine helped to change me a bit. After all, getting up at the crack of dawn every day and exercising wasn't the easiest thing to do, especially on vacation.

Maybe, it also helped me learn to get along with people with different personalities. It wasn't easy living with Heather for the past weeks, and Candy and Helen. Of course, we really tried to avoid them and they tried to avoid us, so I guess that didn't count.

Probably the hardest thing was learning to live with Big B. Not that she was exactly living with us, but close to it. She was in our business every second. Worse than Mother or Dad.

I wondered if Mother planned all of this. That would be just like her. Making my life more difficult. I know she spent several weeks looking for the 'right' camp. She and Dad read several brochures before deciding. I didn't have any say in the decision. Dad said it would be my turn to decide when I had children of my own. I could wait on that one.

I must have dozed off, for the next thing I knew someone had thrown cold water all over me.

"Tracey, are you listening?"

"Who did that?" I sputtered.

"I did. You aren't paying attention. It's like I'm talking to myself," Nancy Ann said sharply.

"You probably were. I must have fallen asleep. Sorry."

"What were you saying?"

"I was wondering what the guys were doing today."

"I remember hearing Paul say something about a ten mile hike."

"Ten miles! Boy, that would be the day you got me on a hike like that one," said Nancy Ann.

"Well, you weren't invited. There is nothing to worry about." I felt myself dozing off again.

"Here, use some lotion," muttered Nancy Ann, breaking into my dream.

"Hey, look at that rope?" said T.

I squinted up into the sunlight. Entangled in a branch of an old weathered looking tree was an even more weathered looking rope.

"I bet it was once used as a swing to jump into the hole," said T. "Let's get it loose."

"Okay, go for it, T," I said.

T frowned at me. Nodding, she proceeded to scale the boulders and climb up the trunk of the tree, her feet digging into the dry bark. Pieces coming off as her toes held on.

"Careful, T," said Nancy Ann.

"I'm glad she volunteered and not me," said Robin.

"Me too," said Bambi.

I looked at Nancy Ann. She smiled back. I couldn't imagine Bambi climbing anything, let alone that dead tree.

T was a regular tom boy. It didn't take her long. The rope fell loose and hung about four feet from the water.

"I don't think it will hold me," said Bambi, "I'll just watch."

"Who's first? Yelled T as she moved downward to a lower level.

"Why you, of course," said Heather. "We want to see how strong it is."

Another frown.

T stood on a platform that was built on a lower branch. She reached far out over the water and grabbed onto the rope.

I looked upward. The platform didn't look too sturdy. Neither did the rope.

But what the heck, it was only water down below.

"Well, here goes nothing," announced T and grabbed the rope tightly.

I looked at Nancy Ann. She had her eyes shut tight. Even in the movies when someone was getting shot at, or a monster was attacking, Nancy Ann would shut her eyes. Well, there was no monster here. And I could see no one shooting at T. But I had an uneasy feeling that I should close my eyes too.

CHAPTER 22

"AH-AH-AH-AH-AH-AH-AH" A TARZAN-LIKE noise echoed around us, bouncing off the boulders like a set of drums. I opened one eye just in time to see T let go of the rope and splash into the water. Except, it was more like a ka-boom. The water sounded hard. Water couldn't be that hard. Or could it?

"Ohhh..."

"What's the matter, T? Belly hurt?" yelled Robin.

"A bit," said T, almost too low to hear.

"Maybe, more than a bit," said Nancy Ann under her breath.

"Yeah," I said smiling. I had shut my eyes again to keep out the blinding sun. This was the life. If it could only remain so peaceful.

"Well, if it isn't the birds. Are you going to get your feathers singed again?" a voice crackled nearby interrupting my space.

"Tracey! It's Helen and Candy."

"That's okay, let's don't pay attention. Maybe, they'll go away."

"Tracey, you're not going to say anything?"

"Nah, they're not worth it." My eyelids remained closed.

"You're probably right. That's what they want."

Dad would have been proud of me. I needed to not let others push my buttons. It's funny how people can get others going by saying something little but nasty.

"Well, who's next?" asked T as she clambered up on Nancy Ann's rock.

"Not me!" said Nancy Ann.

"That water sounded awfully hard," I said.

I opened one eye to look at T's red legs. They must have stung. But knowing T she wouldn't admit it. I probably wouldn't either if I were her.

"Yeah. It felt kind of hard... but the first time is always the worst."

"You mean you're going again?" squealed Nancy Ann.

"I will, but I want someone else to go with me."

"Not enough guts, huh?"

"It's more fun, Tracey, when others want to do crazy things with you. Don't you think?"

Of course, T had to be right. I thought of some of the crazy stunts I had pulled here at camp. They wouldn't have been as much fun if I had done them by myself.

"Yeah, I guess you would call it sharing?"

"Sharing is not only the good times, but also the bad times," said a familiar voice.

"Well, looks like all of bungalow fourteen is here now," I said lifting not only an eyelid but an eyebrow. Heather spread her towel out on a large flat rock two boulders away from us.

"Well, make yourself at home," said T. "There's plenty of sun for all of us."

"But I'm not sure about space," whispered Nancy Ann.

I had nothing to say. Nancy Ann looked at me suspiciously. I think she thought I had something up my sleeve. Except, I had no sleeves on, just a bathing suit.

I turned over hoping my backside would get a little color. I needed to have a nice tan to take back home, since Mother didn't want any more snakes like last year.

Candy and Helen were propped up on the other side of the water hole. I had to admit they both looked pretty good in their bathing suits. Their suits were the newest styles, cut high up over the hips. Mother would never have let me get a suit like that. Dad would have never let me bring one into the house.

"Do you think they shave their legs?" asked Nancy Ann.

Startled, I looked at Nancy Ann. Then I looked down at my own legs. My hair was blond and soft.

"I wonder if it's difficult to shave."

"We could always try," said T who was still sitting on Nancy Ann's rock. The hair on T's legs was dark brown.

"I wonder if it would make me look better in a bathing suit," I said half out loud, but more like a thought to myself.

"I don't have any hair under my arms yet," said Nancy Ann lifting one arm.

"Me either," I said.

"I have a little bit. But not much to speak of," said T.

T had about seven hairs. Not under just one arm, but including both of them.

I laughed. So did Nancy Ann.

"I think it would be a lot easier to start shaving away from home," said T.

"Ditto. Ditto! It's not easy going through any personal changes at home. Your parents are always watching you."

"Let's catch a few more rays and then get back to the bungalow before Candy and Helen to see if they have a razor," whispered T.

"Really?" asked Nancy Ann.

"That's a terrific idea!" I could see Mother's disapproving look if she saw any legs all shaven and smooth.

As I lay on my rock waiting for a time to leave, I could feel an excitement shoot through my body. This was going to be fun. I loved trying new things.

At least, this wouldn't get me into trouble with Big B. And I wasn't getting anyone else into trouble. And no one was getting anyone else into trouble. And no one was getting hurt this time.

CHAPTER 23

"TRACEY! LOOK AT what you're doing!" shrieked Nancy Ann.

"Does it hurt?" asked T sharply, making a squeamish face.

T had been right on target. We had found a razor in Helen's bag, all wrapped carefully in toilet paper. After grabbing the razor, we headed for the bathroom.

We had left everyone back at the hole saying we were going to the canteen to get something to eat. Bambi had wanted to go. The only way she stayed behind was by my promising to bring her back something. It would be a surprise.

Well, my surprise was that there must be a trick to shaving because I was cutting myself left and right. Shaving wasn't very easy. I wondered how Mother did it. I never saw cuts on her legs. It must take a lot of practice.

"Maybe, the blade is dull. I think it takes a sharp razor to cut through the hair," said Nancy Ann as she watched blood dribble slowly down from my knee.

"Maybe. it's too sharp. Or you're going too fast," said T.

"Maybe, you're just nervous," said Nancy Ann.

"Maybe, it's all of the above, but whatever it is, my legs look awful," I said, trying to get my wounds to stop bleeding with pieces of toilet paper. "They don't feel so good either."

"T, get me some more paper. This is not doing it." The toilet paper was saturated. Blood ran down my legs to the yellow tile floor.

"I wonder how long it will take to stop," said Nancy Ann.

"I think you should take a shower," said T. "At least, the water will wash the blood down the drain. We'll clean up the basin and floor."

I didn't argue. I got into the stall and closed the curtain behind me. The warm water felt good.

"Tracey, you'd better use cold water. I read in my health book that cold water will make the blood clot faster than warm water."

Behind the shower curtain I stuck my tongue out and turned the hot water spigot to the right. I hate cold showers.

I looked down at the drain. The water was more of a pink, no longer red.

"It's working, Nancy Ann. My legs are clearing up."

"It sounds like you're talking about a case of acne," said Nancy Ann. We all laughed.

"Well, who's next?" I asked.

The bathroom was quiet.

I opened the curtain, grabbed my towel and got out.

"Hey, who's next? See my legs aren't too bad. With a little bit of sun you will never notice. And remember, T, it was you who said it's more fun to do things together."

T and Nancy Ann looked at each other.

The next twenty minutes both Nancy Ann and T performed surgery on their legs. I wasn't the only one who cut herself, but I was the one who had the most cuts. Probably, because they learned from watching me. But, by the time they were done, we all needed some sun on our legs, not only to heal the cuts, but also, because the shaving must have taken the first layer of skin off and our legs seemed lighter.

"We'd better get some food and head back. They're probably wondering what's happened to us. Especially, Bambi. She'll head a search party looking for us," said T.

"You're right," I said.

"What excuse can we give?" asked Nancy Ann.

"Let's get the razor back to Helen's bag. Hope she doesn't notice it's been used," I said.

My legs felt funny. Not just the cuts. They didn't sting anymore. My legs just seemed emptier. Or rather something felt missing. It sure is a lot of work to become a woman. I wondered if it was all worth it.

I had taken off my watch so as not to get a band mark from the sun. But, I figured we had about three more hours of good sunshine to soak up.

As we walked down to the canteen, I looked at myself in the window of the chow hall. I think my back was straighter. Not that shaving had anything to do with my back, but maybe, I felt a little older.

If Mother notices my legs, she'll notice my posture too, I thought. I'll tell her that shaving helped me stand straighter. More like a lady.

Yes, that was it. I felt more like a lady. This was my first step towards womanhood. I smiled smugly to myself.

CHAPTER 24

"WELL, IT'S ABOUT time!" shouted Bambi as we rounded the last bend in the trail leading to the dammed-up water.

"What did you bring?" asked Robin.

"Red Vines, Hershey's with almonds, Hawaiian Punch, and a bag of tortilla chips," I answered back, my voice dripping with sarcasm.

"What?" said Bambi, her eyes bulging.

"Well, how about trail mix, dry roasted peanuts, and orange juice?" I paused. "Anyone complaining?" I asked.

The only sounds were Helen and Candy giggling off in the distance.

Nancy Ann flopped herself down on her towel. "Oh, that's hard!"

"That's rock, Nancy Ann, not sand," I said as I sat down more carefully on my boulder. "You have to respect things tougher than yourself."

"Well, now who's next?" asked T.

"Are we still on that subject?" asked Nancy Ann.

"It really is fun. I'll go again if you do."

"Come on, Tracey," yelled T getting up off her towel.

"I'm going too," said Robin.

"Me too," said Nancy Ann.

"I'm not," said Bambi.

"No one asked you," said Heather. "I think you're all crazy. Even though it's just water, you could get hurt up there."

"How?" I asked as I got up. I didn't think it could be any worse than cutting my legs a half dozen times.

All Heather had to do was say something negative to egg me on. Nancy Ann got up too!

"Let's go," she said.

The climb up the rocks to the platform was the easiest part. The trunk was another story. It probably would have been better if I had my Nikes on. The bark cut into my toes.

T went first, but I was right behind her. My knees knocked together. I was glad that no one could hear them. At least, no one said anything. Maybe, all their knees were knocking too.

The branch holding the platform was large. Moss hung down over it making it more unappetizing. The dangling rope was attached to a higher branch. I peeked over the platform and looked down. It was a long way down. Maybe, it was just the angle. I took a step back.

"Hey, watch out, Tracey! We're wobbling!" shouted Nancy Ann nervously.

"Hold on to me, Tracey." I grabbed onto T's waist as she reached out to pull the rope in. Nancy Ann was close behind me. A tremor ran under my feet. The platform started vibrating more.

"Be careful, T," I said, I don't think this old platform can hold all of us much longer."

The boards creaked dangerously.

I felt my weight give, as T took hold of the rope. And it gave in the wrong direction.

Nancy Ann let out a short scream.

Seconds later, Robin was the only one left in the tree. T, Nancy Ann and I were tossed into the air, our arms and legs flaring.

It was a long way down. And longer without the rope in hand. I pictured myself Tarzan, actually Jane, swinging out over the jungle. Except, the vine was nowhere around to catch onto.

Pow, I hit the water. If I thought the water was cold before, it was overwhelming now. My entire body went under.

I wondered how deep the hole was. And where was the bottom.

It seemed my lungs were ready to burst. I was caught off guard when I was knocked off and I hadn't taken a deep breath. I just knew I had to get back up to the top.

Minutes later, I was swimming for the shore. Followed by Nancy Ann and T. I thought of Heather in all her glory. I probably should have listened. Darn her.

My nostrils stung. I had swallowed a bunch of water. I choked as I pulled myself up on a river rock and lay there. The sun felt so good.

"Are you guys all right?" asked Bambi as she knelt beside us.

"Yeah, I don't think we need CPR. Thanks for asking," I said.

"Did I ask that?" said Bambi looking doubtful.

"Hey, you all right?" asked Heather looking honestly concerned.

"Yeah, everything under control," said T as she sat up on a rock. "Sorry, guys, for getting you into this."

"Look, how you cut yourselves!" said Bambi. "That fall must have done it! You must have scraped yourselves on the platform!"

I looked at my legs and at T's and Nancy Ann's. They were a mess. But not from the accident. Everywhere I had cut myself was an ugly red mark. Several places, the skin had been scraped off.

"Yeah, well. That bark is really rough," said T.

I looked at T. Then at Nancy Ann. And smiled.

Rough wasn't the word for it. I hoped that it would be easier the next time. Falling from a tree branch was a lot easier and less damaging than shaving.

CHAPTER 25

"OH, TRACEY, MY legs look so much worse this morning. Look!"

Nancy Ann carefully pulled at her pajama leg. It looked like a rash of chickenpox.

"It looks tender!" said T as she crawled over onto the lower bunk.

"It is. Don't get too close," whined Nancy Ann.

"What's happening here?" asked Robin plopping herself down on the hard floor.

Nancy Ann pulled up her pant leg.

"Let me see!" said Robin.

I looked at Nancy Ann. My legs looked and felt just as bad.

Nancy Ann slowly drew her pant leg up.

"Egad! That couldn't have all been caused by the broken platform!"

"Is that a question or a statement?" asked T.

Robin looked at Nancy Ann.

"What's the matter?" asked Bambi sitting up and rubbing her eyes.

"You should see Nancy Ann's legs! Tracey, you too. You're both a mess! What did you do?"

"We sort of experimented," I said meekly.

"Experimented!" said Robin. "Well, your results weren't very good. That rash looks dangerous."

"It's called razor burn," said Heather looking over Robin's shoulder. "I've seen it before, but not so bad. Besides, it must be contagious. Huh, T?"

"Yeah, don't talk too loud. You might wake up the sleeping beauties."

"They don't ever wake up for the bugle. Why worry? What did you do? Get into their razor?" remarked Heather.

"Well, sort of," said Nancy Ann.

"It's either yes or no. There's no in between," said Heather shortly. "It looks like you jerks didn't use soap either!"

"Soap!" Nancy Ann and I chimed in together.

My face must have turned a pretty shade of pink – for both T and Nancy Ann's faces were also glowing.

"Yep. Soap makes it a lot easier to shave."

"Will you guys hold it down over there!" said Helen putting her head under her pillow. "It's too early."

"Okay, okay," said Heather.

Humph, maybe I should change my mind about Heather, I thought. She could easily have told Helen we borrowed her razor. And she didn't.

I looked at Nancy Ann. She was thinking the same thought.

"I'm hungry," said Bambi.

"Me too!" said Robin.

My thoughts turned to breakfast. Poached eggs over toast and a tall glass of orange juice. I hadn't had a donut or a jelly roll in weeks. I wondered if my stomach could adjust to the taste of jelly donuts again. I sure missed them. Maybe, I should change my eating habits. Then, maybe, my hair would grow longer and shinier. Maybe, my nails would be stronger. I could look like a model in one of those fashion magazines. I wondered how long it would take me. First of course, my legs would have to heal. I couldn't very well pose for a leg ad.

"Let's head for the shower, Tracey!" said Nancy Ann.

That sounded good to me and I grabbed my towel. Aerobics had been cancelled this morning.

We had one day of relief.

"Last one to the showers is a rotten egg," said T as she galloped out the door.

As the door slammed behind us, I heard Candy yell at us. I missed the words but got the message. I think it had to do with the screen door.

"What's on the agenda today, ladies?" asked Heather as she tossed a bar of soap over the curtain to Bambi.

"I don't know. What do you think, Tracey?" said Nancy Ann as she rubbed lotion on her legs.

My body felt in good condition. My muscles had stopped aching after the first week. Between aerobics, horses, canoeing, and simply walking for days, my body had run the gamut as far as exercise... wait 'til I tell Sarah. She'll never believe me. Speaking of which, I owed her a letter.

"Let's ask the cook to pack us a lunch and go for a hike," I said.

"A hike?" questioned Nancy Ann.

"A hike. We can handle a good one now." I said.

"What do you mean by a good one?" asked Bambi suspiciously.

"How far is a good one?" asked Nancy Ann, her voice cracking. "I like hiking but I hope you don't mean a ten-mile excursion like the guys went on. We haven't heard from them. They may not have made it back to camp yet."

"You're so funny. Let's time ourselves and go as far as we can for two hours and have lunch and then retrace our footsteps," I said.

"That sounds like a plan to me," said Heather.

What do you know? Heather agreed with me. Maybe, we were all growing a little.

July 22

Dear Diary,

Bet you didn't know that hiking can be dangerous to your health?

Well, it is and it was. My poor feet. Blisters everywhere. I am writing this entry while my feet soak in a bowl of warm water with Epsom salts. Be thankful that my fingers don't have blisters on them, or you wouldn't be hearing from me.

The day was too beautiful to stay in camp so we got out. By we, I mean Nancy Ann, T, Robin, Heather, Bambi, and me. Yes, even Bambi. She did pretty well too. We had to rest a lot for her, but that was okay because we were all tired too.   And we all have become friends.

We just didn't want to admit it.

At breakfast we asked the cook to make us a lunch. She outdid herself.

Sandwiches with cucumbers, bean sprouts, and avocado with a sprinkle of poppy seeds.

Bambi doesn't like avocadoes so she lost out on the sandwiches. She ended up eating six bananas. She'll never lose any weight that way. I wonder if she'll ever try.

The trees here are so enormous that it is difficult to explain just how really big they are. I'm not sure what to compare them to. Or if it is even right to compare them to anything. Being among them is like having a spiritual experience. Not that I'm religious, but I get a special feeling just being around them. It's like I'm in a special place in a special time.

None of us said much as we walked through the woods. We also watched out for animals. Nancy Ann looked for wild flowers. And Heather kept an eye out for poison oak.

It wasn't too long after lunch that Bambi started complaining about a stomach ache. What did she expect! After six bananas.

I bet she never eats bananas again. Daddy says that if a person wanted to get over a bad habit like eating candy, then all you would have to do is overdose one time on it till you get sick. What a way to go! I guess I have never overdosed enough to give anything up.

"Tracey, that water is cold. It won't help your feet anymore," said Robin. The water was no longer warm. After putting my diary down, I reached for a towel and gently wiped around my toes.

"Boy, between your battered legs and your

feet, you need medical attention. Maybe, we should take you to sick bay," said Nancy Ann grinning.

"You're just lucky that your shoes weren't new. Mine weren't broken in enough," I said as I surveyed myself. I was supposed to go home with the new look, tan and slender. The new me. Instead, I looked like I had a run-in with the corner butcher.

CHAPTER 26

"TURN THAT LIGHT off!" snapped someone. I recognized Candy's voice. It was always so proper yet drooled with nastiness. I pointed my flashlight down towards the second page of my letter to Sarah, covering it with the palm of my hand.

"Tracey, don't forget to ask her about her arrival time. Maybe, we could go with Mrs. Browning to the airport."

"Check!" I said.

"Shhh..." whispered Robin.

Whose side was she on anyway? I couldn't get to sleep. My feet still hurt. In fact, they never stopped hurting. I had some of the biggest blisters I had ever seen. I didn't know what I would wear tomorrow.

I couldn't wear my Nikes. And they didn't' like us going barefoot. I guess I would have to wear flip flops.

How I hated flip flops. Just like last year's summer camp. It would be just my luck that I would get blisters between my toes.

The bungalow was really dark. And my

flashlight was really dim. I had left it on for several hours the other night and had wasted it. I didn't feel like replacing the batteries. Batteries cost money. Dad would get more when I got home. It was his flashlight anyway.

I hoped Sarah could read my chicken scratching. I didn't particularly want to write it over again either.

Someone started snoring. Must be Bambi. It was coming from her direction. No one said anything.

Everyone must be asleep.

Well, this place is really dead. Wish Nancy Ann was awake so I could talk to someone. I guess she's really tired from our long hike. I would be too if my feet weren't keeping me awake. I guess I sound like I'm complaining but my feet hurt so much.

Our days are going so fast here. Never a dull moment. We'll be home before you know it. We'll have so much to talk about.

I stopped writing. My thoughts were interrupted by a crackling sound. A shiver went up my spine.

A minute later, I nervously picked up my pen. I didn't like being the only one awake.

I figured my imagination was just working overtime.

I sure would like you to meet my friend Paul. He's very nice. And cute. I hope he'll want to write to me after camp is out. He lives in Southern California. Pretty far away.

I froze. And clicked my flashlight off.

I knew my imagination wasn't working overtime now. The noise I heard was like breaking twigs or crackling leaves.

"Nancy Ann," I whispered.

"Nancy Ann." She could sleep through anything.

I moved my top leg very slowly and then slithered across the top of my bunk. It seemed like it took me a long time to get down to Nancy Ann's bunk.

"What the..." stuttered Nancy Ann.

I tried to put my hand over Nancy Ann's mouth in the dark. "Shhh... listen," I said.

After a silence, Nancy Ann said, "What am I supposed to hear? Bambi, snoring?"

"Lower your voice," I said.

It seemed like someone or something was rubbing itself against our bungalow.

I pictured a giant black bear leaning up against the building. Except, I didn't feel any vibrations.

The noise continued.

"Let's wake up the others," said Nancy Ann meekly.

"Yeah, strength in numbers," I said. At the same time, I didn't want to look like a fool if it was some animal like a raccoon.

"Let's investigate before we get the others up," I said.

Just as I finished speaking, the noise stopped.

"Well, what now?" asked Nancy Ann.

I ignored her and grabbed my flashlight. It would make a good weapon. I felt my nerves coming back.

"Come on," I insisted as I grabbed at Nancy Ann's pajamas.

I stumbled over someone's tennis racket.

Klunk!

Darn those girls!

"What's going on?" asked Heather.

"Something's out there!" said Nancy Ann.

"Whhhat!" said Robin.

Goose bumps rose up on my arms, as I thought of something or someone out there listening to us talk.

Whatever it was, it wasn't making any noises at the moment.

Everyone was awake now. Except for the two who needed their beauty sleep.

"Keep your voices down!" I said a little too loudly.

My flashlight dropped. Darn, I thought.

"Help me find my flashlight," I asked of everyone.

Heads cracked.

"Ohhh," said T.

"My head," said Nancy Ann, rubbing her forehead.

"Here," said Robin turning on the flashlight as she handed it to me. It was really dim now.

"Let's go outside," I said.

"Who's going outside?" said Bambi. "It's better inside."

"Yeah, you don't know what's outside," said Nancy Ann with a high-pitched shiver in her voice.

There were so many delays that whatever was out there would be gone by the time we opened the door.

The door was not so bad. But the screen door squeaked loudly on its hinges. It's funny how I had never noticed that before. Of course, I had never tried to sneak out, either.

T was right behind me. Nancy Ann had fallen behind her.

"Tracey, shine your light over here," prompted T.

The dim light played havoc. I couldn't tell where real objects started and the shadows ended.

It was crazy.

What was I doing out here anyway? I thought. Bambi was right. It was better inside. If not better, it was at least safer. Whatever was out there, would go away sooner or later.

"Let's go back," whined Nancy Ann.

"I think we should take her advice," said T.

I didn't need much prompting.

Everyone was back inside within a minute.

It wasn't till I was sitting back on my bunk that I remembered my tender feet. Darn those pine needles.

Misery.

And just what was out there?

Maybe, a pack of coyotes. Did coyotes come into people's camps like bears did?

"My head really hurts," said T. "I'm going to have a real lump."

"I have a headache!" whined Nancy Ann.

Well, I wasn't the only one hurting now. That made me feel a little better. Now maybe, I wouldn't be the only one who had a difficult time falling asleep.

CHAPTER 27

SOMEHOW, THE MORNING sun managed to wake me up early. Too early. Before, the bugle sounded.

No one stirred but me. No one had anything to say this early.

I didn't have much to say either. I lay in my bunk wondering if I should try my feet out. Or maybe, I should just stay where I was before Big B, in all her morning splendor, woke us up.

Thinking about last night didn't make me very comfortable. I knew someone or something had been out there.

I peeked down at the lower level. Nancy Ann lay on her stomach with her left leg stretched out in the air. Her pajama leg didn't hide her battle scars from the razor.

I couldn't go back to sleep. Not even for fifteen minutes. I pushed my blanket to the side. I couldn't stay in bed any longer. The suspense of last night egged me on. I grabbed onto the ladder and gingerly climbed down. My feet still hurt.

"Where are you going?"

Startled, I looked over in the direction of the voice. Nancy Ann popped her head up. Her rumpled red hair hid one of her eyes.

"I was thinking of taking a look outside," I said.

"What's there to see at this time of the morning?" asked Nancy Ann, yawning.

"Probably nothing... but I want to examine the campground before anyone else gets up."

"Investigation could get you into trouble," said Nancy Ann.

"Me? Trouble? Not me," I said, grinning.

"Well, if you're going. So am I. Let me put my slippers on first."

I carefully put on the flip flops I had borrowed from one of the girls in bungalow twelve.

Why did that darn screen door have to squeak, I thought as we tiptoed out.

Looking back, I saw that we had not disturbed anyone.

"Tracey! Look!"

I turned. My jaw dropped open.

Toilet paper. Everywhere. Someone had decorated the entire area around our bungalow with it. All through the trees. All over the roof. It was quite a remarkable job.

"Wow!"

"That took a lot of time," remarked Nancy Ann.

"And energy," I said.

"Now who do you suppose did that?" said a voice coming from behind me.

I turned to see Big B standing, her legs apart, with her bugle in hand.

I felt insulted. Nancy Ann looked startled.

"Whhhat are you saying?" asked Nancy Ann.

"Just when I thought you two were doing better."

"We..." I started to say. But Big B wasn't going to let me explain.

"You disappoint me. Look at this mess. How are you going to clean it up?"

"We didn't..." I protested. My words being wasted. This was so unfair. I must admit we... I mean... I have pulled a few stunts in my time, but this --.

"How could we have gotten up there?" said Nancy Ann, her voice cracking as she looked up into the trees.

"You didn't," said Big B, a frown making a crease in her forehead.

"But... "

"What's going on?" A head peeked out of bungalow fourteen. Robin's body followed.

"Look at all the tree decorations," said Big B.

Robin didn't have anything to say. She just stared. Everywhere. Rolls and rolls of toilet paper.

"Well, look at that!" said Heather as she slammed the screen door behind her.

"Yeah, pretty, huh?" said Big B. The crease

was getting deeper. "Any suggestions on how it got there?"

"Well, it wasn't any of us," stated Heather matter-of-factly. "Everyone was in bed early."

"No one here could have done that in the dark," said Robin.

"Besides, it's not that big of a thing," said Heather. "Water will dissolve it and wash it down as soon as it rains."

Thank goodness for know-it-all Heather. She could come in handy at times.

But my bubble would burst all too quickly.

"Rain! This is the middle of July! It might not rain 'til November. That is, if we're lucky," snapped Big B.

The screen door opened again. "It's past six-thirty," said Candy. "Are we all sleeping in this morning?"

"Or is your bugle broken?" asked Helen.

Both came out of the bungalow dressed in nightgowns that looked like something out of the Victorian period. Even in the morning, they looked sickeningly gorgeous.

I ran my hand through my tangles. It was hopeless. I would never look that good.

"Well, what's to be done now?" asked Robin.

"I'm going to find out who the culprit is," said Big B, turning away. "But that doesn't leave you two off the hook. I somehow think you two are involved."

With her bugle in hand, Big B tramped off to the hilly part of the camp.

It was not until breakfast was finished did Big B make the announcement:

"Whoever had valid proof of who decorated the camp with toilet paper will earn the choice of a large pizza at Mountain Jack's."

"Well, we're making progress. It's not a vegetarian delight this time," said Robin.

"Yeah, who's going to fink on anyone for a rabbit-food pizza?" said Bambi, stuffing her mouth with her last bite of toast heaped with a fried egg.

Bambi then proceeded to let out a belch.

"That is so disgusting," whispered Nancy Ann from behind me.

I nodded, as I thought of the times I burped, and how both my Dad and Mother jumped on me.

It all depended on who got to me first. Once, they yelled at me at the same time.

I must admit I didn't find Bambi's table manners very appetizing.

"Well, what are we going to do about the toilet paper?" said T. "It sounded like Big B wanted us to get it down."

"Yeah, but how?" asked Nancy Ann.

"I have a thought," I said.

"Oh, oh... I don't like the sound of your thought," said Heather.

"No, it's like what you were saying. Water will dissolve it. Right?"

"R-R-Right! But it's July," said Heather.

"Well, water comes in other forms. What if we washed it down with water from a hose?" I said, thinking that my idea was a good one.

"Maybe, one of those really big hoses."

"You mean using a high-powered hose nozzle!" said Heather.

"Where are we going to find such a thing?" asked Robin, her eyes growing wide.

"Hmmm... at a fire station" said T. "They have high-powered hoses."

"But those hoses are too high powered!" stated Heather, "Besides, no one here could handle it."

"Maybe, Big B could," said Nancy Ann comically.

"But I don't think we should involve her," I said.

"No, Tracey's right. She wouldn't approve. She never approves of what we do," said Nancy Ann.

"Then, we've got to find some other way," said T.

"How about the hardware store?" asked Robin. "There's one down the block from Mountain Jack's."

"How much do they cost?" asked Nancy Ann, shoving a hand into her pocket. Two dimes and a quarter fell out.

"I don't have much money left," said T, cracking the knuckles on her left hand.

"Do you have to do that?" asked Robin.

"If we pool our money, we should be able to get one," I said.

"Now how are we going to get to town without anyone finding out?" asked Nancy Ann.

My mind was whirling. Another responsibility.

"Come on, guys, let's get our money together. First things first. Getting there will be our next challenge."

CHAPTER 28

"HITCHHIKE!" SAID ROBIN.

"That's ridiculous!" said Heather.

"You are taking a stupid risk doing that! I've heard of some awful stories," said T.

"Tracey, they're right. Your parents would kill you," said Nancy Ann.

"But how else are we going to get there? It's a long walk into town. At least five miles," I said, looking at the money lying on the bed in front of me.

"Yeah, but compare five miles with the rest of your life," said T.

"Well, if it is two or three of us going, what could possibly happen?" I said, not looking at any of them.

"What if there are two or three?" said Heather with a sarcastic twinge in her voice.

"Does anyone have any other suggestions about getting ourselves to town without announcing it to everyone?" I asked.

"Well, then if no one wants to go with me… I'll get the nozzle myself." I gathered up the money, hoping $4.58 was enough.

"We can't let Tracey go by herself," said T.

No one said anything as I got up to get my hoodie. I glanced at my watch. It wasn't quite ten o'clock yet. Plenty of time.

"Let's draw straws..." said Heather. "That will make it fair all the way around."

"I'll get some twigs outside," said Nancy Ann who seemed more than happy to leave the situation.

Some friend, I thought. You would think she would've stood by me. Nancy Ann always did before. Oh well.

"The longest twig goes with Tracey!" said T.

No one was eager to pick a twig. As each girl picked a short stick, her face showed relief.

With some hesitation, Nancy Ann picked a twig.

The twig looked short. It wasn't till we compared all the sticks that we discovered that Nancy Ann chose the longest one.

Nancy Ann wasn't thrilled, but said nothing.

"Come on, we need to get going," I said.

Outside, while putting on a windbreaker, Nancy Ann said, "Honestly, Tracey, do you think we're doing the right thing? We've never done anything like this before. My Mom would really be angry with me."

"How will she ever find out?" I commented. I felt in my pockets for the banana and pear that I had retrieved from breakfast this morning.

We didn't have enough money to eat lunch and dinner wasn't served till five-thirty.

Nancy Ann was silent as we walked in between the bungalows up to the road that led to the main highway.

The camp seemed too silent for mid-morning. Even the birds were quiet. Probably my imagination, I thought.

It was a long way down the gravel road. Nancy Ann didn't say much of anything. In fact, I had never seen her so quiet.

"What are you thinking about, Nancy Ann?"

"You know what I'm thinking about, Tracey."

"Yeah, no matter how you look at it, we're in trouble. Big B thinks we had something to do with the toilet paper. We're already in trouble unless we clean up the mess. Our reputation is being ruined with unfair slander," I retorted.

"Anyway, nothing is going to happen to us," I said with a huff.

The road wound around the mountain. No car passed us. In fact, there was no traffic in any direction. It took us a good thirty minutes to get to the highway. And it was all up hill.

"Let's rest for a few minutes," said Nancy Ann as she sat down on a large rock.

I agreed by sitting also.

Five minutes later we took the turn to the left towards town.

"You know all this walking doesn't help my blisters any," I said.

"This was not my idea, remember?"

My feet hurt. And no cars.

"If I ever walk another mile..." I muttered to myself.

A car... a car was coming. I could hear it around the bend.

"Tracey, what do we do now?"

"Just put your thumb out. It's easy."

The truck was bright yellow. What an awful color, I thought. But the color didn't matter. We needed to get to town. And to the hardware store.

The truck slowed down, "Where are you two going?" asked the driver.

"Er-r-r, we need to get to town," I said, and I realized at that moment that I had regrets about the whole situation.

"It isn't very far at all," the man said. "Hop in."

The truck was high off the ground. In order to climb up, I had to first climb onto the step-up.

Nancy Ann followed.

We sat close together near the door. I wasn't very comfortable. Nancy Ann must have felt worse with a metal armrest sticking into her side. I glanced over. She held a tight grip on the door handle. Her knuckles were white. I tried not to look at the man directly. But out of the corner of my left eye I could see a long scraggly beard, mostly gray. His hair needed cutting badly; and he chewed feverishly on something which I suspected was tobacco. Every so often between words, he would spit out the window. Gross. I rolled my eyes as I thought about our plight.

As we clattered down the road in the clunky yellow truck, the man kept talking.

"What are you girls up to going to town? Taking your chances hitchhiking and all, don't you think? But you young'uns... you've got some strange notions now-a-days." He kept on talking. And he talked about everything: how he had lived up in these parts all of his life; about his wife passing some years back; how the area has changed with vacation people building new homes; how sometimes, the camp called him to work on the plumbing when things went wrong. He chewed on his tobacco and didn't skip one word; while chewing, spitting out the window every-once-in-a while as he hit a period.

My stomach felt awful. I knew it was nerves. But it hurt.

I suppose it would have been worse if the man had not said anything. Silence can be really scary. But the man driving the bright yellow truck kept right on talking.

CHAPTER 29

"**WELL, HERE YOU** are, girls. The hardware store. Hope you find what you're looking for. It was good to have someone to talk to."

I bet he gets pretty lonely, I thought. I nudged Nancy Ann all too quickly as she opened the door of the truck.

The door was stuck. "You have to give that door a real shove to open it," said the man to Nancy Ann. The man reached across me and gave the door a firm push. I sucked my breath in, hoping I would sink further into the seat. But the seat, being of old leather, didn't bulge.

"There you are!" said the man. Nancy Ann almost fell out the door. With me behind her.

"Thank you very much for the ride... we appreciate it very much," I said, giving the door a hard slam.

The yellow truck backed up and then took the turn around the next corner. I stood watching it as it disappeared from view.

"Tracey." Here it goes, I thought.

"Tracey, I just want you to know I'm soaked. I think I used up every bit of sweat that my body has."

"Yeah, me too," I said as I sat down on a bench in front of the hardware store. I really didn't want to go through that again. "Maybe, we should try walking back."

"Yeah, five miles isn't too bad. Boy, do I smell awful," said Nancy Ann as she lifted an arm to her nose.

"Let's find that nozzle and get back to camp. We have a way to go." I felt my blisters. They were going to have neighbors by the time we got home.

The hardware store owner was more than nice. Besides finding the nozzle for us, he gave me enough band-aids to cover all my blisters. At least, my feet would have a chance now.

Almost two hours later, we left the main highway, taking the road into camp. I was limping now. At one point in our uphill hike, it crossed my mind to put my thumb out. But my stomach wouldn't let me go through that ordeal again. We were lucky that that man in the old yellow truck was so nice.

Next time, we might not have such good fortune. Nancy Ann and I lost another five pounds of sweat and I added at least six more blisters to my feet. My parents will never understand when I tell them I needed to come home just so I could relax and get my body back in shape.

All the girls except for Candy and Helen, who were on the tennis courts, were waiting for us.

Robin had made us meatloaf sandwiches from the lunch menu. We were starving. They tasted good with sesame seeds, bean sprouts, and lettuce. I ripped open four packets of catsup and poured it on.

"Camping sure can make me thirsty," said Nancy Ann as she took a gulp of milk before falling upon her sandwich.

"Well, tell us about your experience," said T. "I can't imagine you guys thumbing for a ride."

"Yeah, were you nervous?"

"Who picked you up?"

"Questions, questions. Can't you let us eat first?" I said, my mouth full of bean sprouts.

"Eat in peace," said T. "We'll get the story later. Anyway, here's a note for you."

"Note?" I said.

"Yeah, it came by carrier pigeon," said T.

"No, it didn't," said Robin. "While we were out swimming today, Paul and Charlie managed to sneak over to the hole."

"We missed them!" I said as I thought about the dangling toilet paper and the job we still had to tackle."

"Yep, but read your note," said Bambi, handing me a folded piece of paper after T gave it to her.

Tracey, Nancy Ann,

Meet you behind the stables this evening after supper. Sorry, we missed you today.

Paul, Charlie

Boy, I was a mess. It's a good thing Paul didn't see me in a bathing suit with my legs all destroyed. Probably, just as well, things worked out as they did.

"Come on, Nancy Ann, let's wash down the toilet paper."

I put the note in my pocket, making sure it wouldn't fall out, and headed towards our bungalow.

Everyone followed and minutes later we had hooked up the hose nearby and had screwed on the nozzle.

Nancy Ann and I took turns. My arms got tired of holding the hose in the air. In fact, everyone had a turn. Including Bambi. And Bambi ended up taking over. She was really strong. Washing down the toilet paper was an easy job for her.

"Hey, what's going on?" Oh, oh. Big B, I thought.

"We're cleaning up this mess," said Robin.

"Where did you get that nozzle? That's not from camp," asked Big B.

"Er, we managed," I said. Explanations about certain situations never sounded right.

"Well, maybe just as well, I don't know. As long as the job is getting done." She looked satisfied at the turn of events. Water was falling everywhere. "Maybe, I misjudged you ladies, but I still want the guys who did this."

Has anyone said anything, yet?" asked Heather.

"No, not yet. But I'm sure someone will. After all, who's going to turn down that pizza?"

I looked at Nancy Ann and then at the others.

"Keep up the good work, ladies," said Big B. She left us getting wetter and wetter as the spray fell all around us.

"Gosh, Tracey, we haven't talked to, let alone seen, Charlie and Paul for three days," said Nancy Ann, as she stuffed herself with turkey pie, a piece of crust falling into her lap.

Darn those peas, I thought. Why did they always have to put them in turkey pies... in fact, any kind of meat pies. And eggplant. Little pieces of eggplant in between the peas – Ugh! "Well, we would have seen them today, except for our trek into town."

"We can see what they've been up to when we meet them tonight. T, can you pass me the rest of the grapes since they're just sitting there."

I shoved them into my pocket, thinking I would get hungry later or maybe, I would share them with Paul. It was a nice feeling to kind of like someone, and I hoped he liked me too.

Nancy Ann lowered her voice, "Maybe, we should get going. I want to clean up."

I thought of all the showers I had taken lately. More than I ever had at home. Maybe, I was just getting dirtier here at camp.

"Me too," I said. I sure could use a shower. I also want to soak my feet for a while. These babies are still really tender."

We got up from the table, pushing the bench back.

"What's your hurry?" asked Heather, who was sitting at the end. "You're going to miss dessert."

"I think I'll pass on the frozen yogurt tonight. I'm full," I said, patting my stomach.

"Ah... ha. I bet. It's that hot date you have?"

"Not so loud!" snapped Robin. "Do you want to get them in trouble."

"Not me," said Heather, smiling and rolling her eyes to the side.

I thought about what Heather had said as Nancy Ann and I walked back to the bungalow. Date!

And a hot date, at that! I had never thought of meeting a friend as a date. But maybe, Heather was right.

What would Dad think? And Mother say? I wondered how much trouble I would be in if they knew.

"Nancy Ann, would you think of this as a date?"

"What! Just us and Charlie and Paul?"

"Yeah, what else would I be talking about?"

"No, I don't think so. Dates mean getting dressed up and going out somewhere. And I don't think our parents would let us yet."

"Besides, I'm not sure Charlie and Paul would think of us as dates... maybe, just friends."

I wondered about that.

"Maybe, we will be more than friends."

"Like boyfriend and girlfriend?" asked Nancy Ann.

"Well... at least... I'm not sure. Maybe, I'm just talking."

"We'll have to find out before we go home."

"Here's you soap, Nancy Ann." I tossed the bar of soap into the air.

"Good catch!"

"Good throw," said Nancy Ann, grinning.

Life was looking up, I thought as we headed out of bungalow fourteen, the screen door slamming behind us.

CHAPTER 30

"I WISHED THEY'D picked a better spot," said Nancy Ann as she stumbled down the pathway to the stables.

It wasn't easy. But it seemed like nothing ever was. The path was a well-worn horse trail, very narrow in parts. It was probably okay for horses with their tall legs, but not for us humans.

At that same moment, my can of insect repellant fell out of my back pocket, rolling down among some rocks. "Wait, Nancy Ann!"

"What?"

"It's my bug spray!"

"And?"

"It's down there!"

"I hope that isn't poison oak," said Nancy Ann, whimpering.

"It can't be. That bush looks different. But then I'm not an expert on plants. You're good with flowers. Don't you know plants, too?"

"No, just flowers I collect and press. I think you'd better get a stick. The can is way down inside."

"Hmmm..." I looked around.

"Why did you have to bring that with you tonight, anyway?"

"It's those darn mosquitoes! The night of the camp social, I found one of them sucking on my arm. I don't want any more sores on me."

"But it smells so awful. What would Paul say if he got a good whiff of that?"

"Well, I brought this too." I pulled out of my other back pocket a bottle of cologne, showing it to Nancy Ann.

"L'Air du Temps? I never heard of that!"

"Neither had I, but it must be good. It's Candy's."

"That doesn't make it good... Boy, it smells strong. It must be her mother's. Besides, it says perfume, not cologne."

"I'm not sure I like its smell. It's almost as bad as the insect repellant. I didn't have time to test it. Besides, I didn't want to smell up the bungalow with it."

"Good thinking," said Nancy Ann as she twisted a skinny branch off of the nearest tree. "Here, try this."

I poked and dug into the bush. The plant didn't look inviting. "Those little white flowers might look nicely pressed, Nancy Ann, don't you think?"

"Nah, they're too sticky-looking."

Nancy Ann grabbed onto my waist and I reached further in.

"Hold on!" and with that my stick hit the can of spray. The can went flying. And so did we.

"Ahh-hhh".... Right into the middle of the bush.

It seemed like pain shot through every exposed pore of my body. And even in some pores that were covered.

"Help, Tracey!" Nancy Ann groaned. "I'm burning!"

"What's all the noise?" It was Paul's voice.

"We're over here," I moaned.

"What did you two get yourselves into?" said Charlie, pulling Nancy Ann to her feet.

"A mess!" said Nancy Ann, her voice quivering. "A real mess! And I hurt! I feel like I've been stung by a hive of bees."

"You fell into a Nettle Bush! Think you two need to cool off? That will help with the stinging," said Paul. "Let's go down to the lake and splash water on you."

I was feeling miserable. "My can of repellant!"

"What?" said Charlie.

"Get my can of repellant, Charlie. It's over there."

"That thing caused this whole predicament," said Nancy Ann.

"Let's go around this way," said Paul, grabbing my hand. "It's a short cut."

Maybe, this is all worth it, I thought. My hand felt good, snug in Paul's. I didn't even say a word as his grip pressed into one of my cuts on a finger. I was afraid he might let go.

"Over here," said Paul to Charlie and Nancy Ann.

"Boy, you two can really get into situations. You have a knack for it," smiled Paul.

Now, normally I would have a come-back, but I couldn't think of a thing to say. The hurt took all of the energy out of my soul.

Suddenly, I was slipping. Paul had let go of my hand.

"What... the!" I said surprised.

Paul was sitting on the ground.

"What happened?" said Charlie.

"I... er... slipped," said Paul.

Not only had Paul slipped into a pile of horse dung, but he also was sitting in it.

"Oh, my goodness," said Nancy Ann.

I thought that was a nice way to say it. Suddenly, I forgot my hurting body. I looked at Paul, who was not moving very fast out of the horse manure. Laughter took over. Not only did he look ridiculous, but he smelled awful.

"I think you need to rinse off too," I said. "We're not the only ones who seem to get ourselves into a mess. But our messes are usually a little less smelly."

I didn't feel like giving Paul my hand. I didn't volunteer.

"Let's get going," said Paul. "I need to wash up."

"Well, we don't want to go too fast," said Charlie. "We would like to watch where we're stepping. I think the horses have left us their calling cards. But, if you want to go ahead, don't wait for us. We'll be okay."

I looked back at Charlie and Nancy Ann. Charlie held onto Nancy Ann's arm. He probably didn't want her to fall into any horse traps. If Paul hadn't let go of my hand, I would have ended up just like him. And I know that mud can cool off bee stings, but I'm not sure about horse dung cooling off nettle stings. I had my doubts.

"We only have three more days left," said Paul.

The feel of the water lapping up on my legs was refreshing. Once we had gotten to the lake, we had gone in clothes and all. I just wanted to feel the coolness of the water on my skin. My hoodie hung heavy on me, but I didn't care. I played with several blades of grass that had grown in between the rocks we were sitting on.

"What are you going to do for the rest of the summer?" asked Paul.

"Rest of the summer? Well, I don't know. Mom can always find stuff for me to do." Now that was a stupid thing to say, I thought. "Nancy Ann and I always find different things to get into." I rattled on. I sounded like I was nervous. I was.

"Doesn't sound too exciting," said Paul.

"Well, what about you?" I asked. I bet he had plenty to keep him busy. He must have a lot of friends; Paul's probably really popular with the girls, too.

Paul's hair was damp and the curls hung further down in his eyes. He had the prettiest hair.

I should be so lucky. Maybe, a new hair cut would improve my looks.

I thought about the L'Air du Temps in my back pocket. But it would look funny, putting it on now. My timing was off.

But maybe, that was part of my charm. Charm... I wondered if I had any.

Paul talked of being on the basketball team at school and how he practiced all the time. He and Charlie had lived in the same neighborhood ever since Paul could remember and they were on the same team. It kept them pretty busy.

In between the girls, I thought.

Well, look at me. I'm jealous. I've never thought about things like that before. That's so crazy.

"Will you be coming to camp next year?" said Paul, breaking into my thoughts.

I glanced at Nancy Ann. She and Charlie must be having quite a conversation. They laughed more than they talked.

"Ah... sure... probably. Nancy Ann and I

really had a good time this summer." I felt I could speak for both of us. Nancy Ann looked like she was having a great time. "It felt good being in an aerobics program with all the healthly food to go with it." I thought about my eating habits at home. The most exercise I ever got was walking to school or climbing around the creek. I guess my life was due for a change.

"Well... maybe we could keep in touch till then. We're coming back next year. This is our second summer here."

I wondered who Paul had met last year.

"You're the first girl I have made friends with."

"Really?"

"Yeah, the girls are always into their own thing, but you seem different than the rest of them."

It was at that moment in the conversation that my heart stopped beating. I took one of my broken nails and poked the palm of my hand. "Oh..."

"What's the matter?" asked Paul.

"Those nettle things still hurt," I was glad the sun going down didn't show off the color on my face. My face felt warm. And my head whirled.

This must be love, I thought. I didn't feel so good. My stomach felt sick. Maybe, I was just nervous.

But it had to be more than that, for it was less than a minute later that I was upchucking.

CHAPTER 31

"THAT'S NOT LOVE!" said Robin. "You're goofy!"

"Your body reacted to the nettle poisoning," said Heather.

"Then how come I didn't get it?" asked Nancy Ann.

"Everybody is different," said Heather.

"Besides, love is more than your body getting sick," sighed Robin.

"How would you know?" said T as she tossed her long hair over her shoulders and pulled at a knuckle.

I wondered why Paul didn't go for someone like T. She was really pretty. My hair would never look like that. And look at my nails. And scars. And blisters. And my body was ill. I was in no condition for someone to like me.

"Well... I've looked at some of my mother's books and the closest to sickness is when the heroine faints. Nettle poisoning is a little bit heavier."

It was getting late and I was tired. It had

been a long day. Too long. I should have written in my diary, but that would have to wait.

Sarah will never believe that right in the middle of the greatest love scene of my life, I threw up; then maybe, she would.

Thank goodness I missed Paul. But the mess careened over the rocks. The second time was in the grass as I clambered down. Paul had followed.

It didn't take us long to get back to camp. We avoided the riding stables because we couldn't see the trail very well. It had gotten dark before we realized it.

I made a feeble excuse and said goodnight as we parted company on the outskirts of the girls' camp. That night had to be the most embarrassing moment in my life.

"Tracey, how are you feeling?" asked Nancy Ann.

"Are you asking in regard to my stomach, or my heart?" I said. I was not sure that I hurt only because of my physical condition.

I was positive Paul would never have anything more to do with me. If I were him, I wouldn't have.

"Tracey?"

"Oh, I'm okay," I mumbled.

"You don't sound okay," whispered Nancy Ann.

"How would you feel if you had just thrown up over someone you liked? Paul is the most adorable guy in the world and I blew it!"

"Paul will understand. He knew you weren't feeling well."

I didn't say anything. He never will want to see me again, let alone like me.

Later, I pretended I was asleep so that Nancy Ann wouldn't talk anymore. I needed to think.

I must have slept through the bugle. I hadn't heard a thing.

"Wake up, Tracey! It's time to get up!" said T. Nancy Ann was already sitting on the edge of her bunk, looking sleepy-eyed.

"Can't I pass on aerobics this morning? I'm not up to it."

"You might get away with it, but if Big B finds out where you went last night and what happened to you, you might have to pay the consequences," retorted Heather.

Heather was right. Nancy Ann and I could be in trouble. And with only two days left before Saturday, I didn't want to fall into that pit.

"Groundhogs! Are you coming?" Big B's voice boomed outside.

"Here we come!" said T as she clambered out with Robin and Bambi following.

"Here, Tracey!" said Nancy Ann as she threw me a pair of tights.

I hoped I wouldn't feel this terrible all day. Even the eggs didn't look very appetizing.

"Not eating this morning?" asked Big B from behind me. "You don't look very well, Tracey."

"You'd better eat something," whispered Robin.

I stared at the hot cereal. It looked like granola sprinkled with dates, walnuts, and raisins. I imagined them as insects – beetles, potato bugs, and crickets. My stomach lurched.

"There's extra wheat germ and bran in there to help get you going today," said Big B, smiling.

Big B helped herself to several dishes of hot cereal and a plate of eggs.

Bambi looked at her tray and then at Big B's tray. She then reached for a second dish of cereal.

I wasn't sure if I would get half of this down.

Orange juice. Maybe, the cold juice would pick me up.

Nancy Ann helped herself to a warm bran muffin, two poached eggs and soy bacon.

I don't think I will ever eat breakfast again. But Big B was standing right there...

I sat down on the bench. "What are you thinking about, Tracey?" asked Nancy Ann in between bites of her muffin.

"I'm thinking about what to do with this cereal. My stomach is not going to handle it this morning."

"Why don't you slip it to Bambi?" whispered Nancy Ann.

That was a good idea. I just wasn't thinking very well. I looked around. Big B was standing off to one side, talking to the girls from bungalow six.

"Bambi... Bambi." I shoved the cereal over to her. Bambi just smiled and kept eating.

"Okay, ladies. Before activities, we're spring cleaning your bungalows. Everybody ready?" shouted Big B.

Groans, yawns, and a few words of discouragement were heard throughout the mess hall.

I had forgotten about the work schedule. Getting under those bunks and looking for fuzz balls wasn't my idea of fun.

Big B walked around to the various tables assigning tasks.

You learn how to keep your head down and look at the ground when someone wants you to do something you don't want to. Well, my eyes seemed to bore a hole onto my empty tray.

I just wasn't up for any work this morning.

"Tracey, Nancy Ann, since you've practiced so much on the bathrooms, why don't you take the bath-shower duty?" said Big B pointedly.

I wondered if that was a question or an order, and if we had any other option.

"Yuck!" said Nancy Ann, too loudly.

My day was starting out badly.

It's funny how voices echo in a shower. Even if you are talking low.

"Inspection will be in two hours!" The voice boomed loudly. The words were enough to strike fear into the hearts of even the bravest campers at Camp Sugar Pine.

What seemed like hours later, Nancy Ann and I stood at attention along with the rest of bungalow fourteen. My hands felt rough. That cleaner was hard stuff. I should have worn the large gloves.

Mrs. Scarfield was talking. Something about appreciation for the job we just finished doing.

"...and you, as capable young women whose lifestyle reflects a love of the outdoors and people, communication skills, responsibility, and an enthusiasm for living. We know how important role-modeling is so we selected only those girls..."

Boy, I was still tired. I hoped Mrs. Scarfield's speech would not go on forever.

"Think she's getting sentimental now that camp is almost over," whispered Robin.

"Sounds mushy to me," said T pulling on a knuckle.

"Shhh," said Helen. "T, do you have to do that?"

"Yep!"

I thought of lying down by the water hole, face down, eyes shut. All day. With no one bothering me.

Good idea. I'll make that suggestion to Nancy Ann. My body needed healing. I had only hours to get back into shape.

"Come on, Bambi. You're coming with us. Get your stuff," said Heather.

I had already grabbed my towel and was waiting patiently outside, sitting on a bench. Actually, I was too tired to spend any extra energy.

Candy and Helen had already left, passing by and not even giving me a nod. They were such pills I thought. They may look good, but they didn't act kind.

Those long smooth legs of theirs in their skimpy bathing suits didn't add to their personalities.

Self-centeredness under-minded their good looks. They laughed and giggled till they were out of sight.

They probably did all of that for my benefit. I bet they didn't have any real friends except each other.

I wondered if I would see Paul today. I guessed not, after last night. Oh well... I've heard about summer romances. They never lasted long – according to Robin, such things were only temporary.

But I wished mine would last more than one evening.

CHAPTER 32

I LAY EXHAUSTED on the rock. The sun bearing down on the water hole had gone to my head. My eyes closed. Nancy Ann was saying something about her legs getting more sun. I was thinking about her freckles and how they might all come together and be one big suntan. I must have giggled because I heard her ask me why was I laughing.

I couldn't open my mouth to answer. I was really tired.

Had I put my lotion on? I couldn't remember. Nancy Ann wouldn't have let me forget that.

I was in another place looking down at the water hole. Everyone was there. No one was swimming yet. Just talking. Except for me. My energy had evaporated. It was strange watching the whole scene. Nancy Ann was putting lotion on Robin. She didn't need much, being so tiny.

Bambi had sneaked a bran muffin out of the chow hall. She was picking out the dates and giving them to T.

Heather was reading a book. I couldn't see

the title, but knowing Heather, it probably had to do with facts about something or another. She picked up so much information along the way. She kept everything she read in her head. That sure would make taking tests a whole lot easier down the road.

Candy and Helen were off by themselves as usual. Today, they had on new bathing suits. At least new to me. They had on bikinis. And looked gorgeous. They were gathered tight on the hips and didn't leave much to the imagination. One day I hoped my shape would be that good.

I was looking at Candy when I noticed something peculiar. Her stomach wasn't flat. Well, it was flat but her tummy button hole wasn't. I came in closer for a better look. I couldn't believe what I saw.

It stuck out and looked like an insect coming out of its cocoon. I felt for mine. My stomach button was shaped perfectly. Nice, round and not too deep. Hmmm... Candy shouldn't be wearing bikinis. Her belly button is not one of her better assets. Mother would have made her wear a one-piece.

"Tracey, what on earth are you mumbling about? You're going to get burned if you don't turn over," said Nancy Ann.

"Huh?" I said groggily.

"Boy, the sun really gets to you, huh?" remarked T.

I looked up. I was still lying on my rock. I really had been in another world. I looked over at Candy and Helen. But no matter how I stretched my neck, I couldn't see Helen's stomach. She had put on a T-shirt. Darn, I thought.

"Tracey, what's the matter?" asked Nancy Ann.

"I'm not sure."

"You're talking in riddles," retorted Nancy Ann.

"Yeah, maybe I am. It's probably the sun. It's getting hot out here." I looked down at the back of my legs. They were getting red.

"Here, put more sunscreen on," said Robin.

"I won't get a dark tan that way."

"You won't get a burn either," said Heather as she looked up from her reading.

My legs were healing. Mother would never notice all my razor cuts by the time I got home.

Next time, I would do a better job. I would also use soap first.

"Well, what's for lunch?"

I turned my head around. I thought I recognized that voice. Paul and Charlie stood a bit away with their suits on. Paul looked terrific!

Robin whispered something to Bambi... too low for me to hear. She laughed and I could feel my face get red. I glanced over at Nancy Ann. She had been in the middle of putting on a wrap and froze.

"Well, what's for lunch?" asked Charlie.

"Er, we just brought some fruit with us from

breakfast," said Nancy Ann, pulling her top up higher.

"Doesn't sound too awfully filling. Want to come with us?" asked Paul, looking at me. "Maybe, we can find some junk food."

"Junk food?" said Bambi, who usually never says much around Charlie and Paul.

"Well, sort of. We're having a cookout for lunch today. What if we were to bring you back hamburgers?" said Paul, smiling... his curls falling across his forehead.

"Real ones?" asked Bambi, excitedly.

"Real ones? What other kind are there?" asked Charlie.

"You don't want to hear the answer to that!" I said.

"Come on, Tracey. We need some assistance bringing them back." Paul reached out for my hand, helping me up.

I looked over at Candy and Helen. They had stopped talking. They didn't miss a thing. I had hoped they wouldn't.

I guess Paul had forgotten about last night. He didn't mention one thing about the mishap except if I was feeling better.

I couldn't believe how perfect the day was. Nothing was going to go wrong. I still wore the flip flops I had borrowed. I hoped Paul didn't notice them. In fact, I hoped he didn't notice any of my mistakes.

It didn't take us very long to get to the boys' camp. We waited on the outskirts while Charlie and Paul loaded themselves down with the provisions.

Fifteen minutes later, Paul and Charlie carrying three large bags found us picking wild strawberries.

"Here's our dessert," I said handing Paul one of the berries.

"Well, we have hamburgers, potato salad, chips, and we even got punch," said Paul.

"Super!" said Nancy Ann, squealing. "You're going to have friends for life."

"We hope so," said Charlie. Nancy Ann's face went red.

Gosh, it sure was nice liking someone and being liked back. I had so much to tell Sarah when we all got back together.

July 26

Dear Diary,

I had the best day... we had a picnic at the old water hole and Paul and Charlie brought the food. We ate so much! But I didn't eat as much as I wanted to. It's funny how you can lose your appetite when you least expect it. I managed to eat half of a hamburger piled with lots of relish, tomatoes, lettuce, pickles, but no onions.

We swam the rest of the day. Paul is really terrific. He can make me laugh at the littlest things. It's too bad he lives in the other part of the state. But we are going to stay in touch.

He asked me today if I would text him when I got home. I will get my cell phone back then. No more restrictions for me.

I think Candy and Helen's egos were really messed up today. They avoided us as usual and we avoided them. But I bet they would have liked to have joined us. They missed out on all the fun, especially when more of the guys from the camp came over.

We had a great game of water ball – more action than I've had since the baseball game. Boys won. But that's okay. I didn't mind. It was fun just being around Paul.

I'm glad I had my own bathing suit on and not the daring ones that Candy and Helen wore. At least, mine stayed in place during the game. With my luck wearing their suits, I would have lost it in between a ball pass.

Paul stayed up to supper time. We agreed to meet tomorrow since it would be our last day here.

I'll call you when I get home from camp.

CHAPTER 33

"WHAT ARE YOU looking at, Tracey?" said Nancy Ann.

"My stomach!"

"Are you afraid of gaining weight? I see no pudges around your waist."

"I'm looking at my tummy button. I have a nice one, don't you think?"

"Tracey, have I ever told you, you can be strange at times?"

"No, but I mean it. I do have a nice one. In fact, it's probably one of my best features."

Nancy Ann bent down to get a better look. "Yes, it probably is, but how often will you be able to display it in public?"

"T, what can I do with my hair to give it a newer look?" I said as I continued to survey myself in the full-length mirror which hung behind the door.

"First, how about giving it a good brushing. And then conditioning it. The sun is drying it out."

"But, I also want to do something different."

"Something for Paul to look at?" snickered Robin.

"But of course," said Nancy Ann as she looked at herself.

"T, do you think you could give me a trim?"

"Sure, if I had a pair of scissors."

I looked at everyone. "Well?"

No scissors.

"But I bet we could get a pair from the infirmary," said Heather.

I have learned to appreciate Heather with her head full of knowledge.

After gulping down breakfast, Nancy Ann and I went over to the infirmary to borrow the scissors.

Mrs. Scarfield was there. She was more than nice. I bet she was going to miss us. We promised to bring the scissors right back and headed back to the bungalow.

"Groundhogs, what are you two up to today? Anything special?" Big B's voice boomed as we walked past the mess hall.

"Oh nothing, except saying goodbyes to everyone and packing," I said.

"Well, it's good to see you're right on top of things. Let me know if there's anything I can do to help you."

That was the person who was going to miss us the most, I thought. Big B was hard on the outside. Big voice, big body, big everything. The picture of meanness but down deep inside, I felt she really liked us. If nothing else, we were a challenge. And we did keep her life exciting.

T had an expert cutting hand. Pieces of hair flew in all directions. I didn't dare look down at the hair on the ground till she was finished. I was going to be a whole new person by the time I left camp.

Twenty minutes later, my hair was short and wavy. With a bit of blow drying, the waves were brushed upward, creating a halo effect around my face. It looked great. I sure hoped Paul thought so too.

"Do me too!" said Nancy Ann.

As T cut Nancy Ann's hair, it got curlier and curlier. Curls bobbed all over her head. She looked like a doll. I bet Charlie really likes her, I thought. Nancy Ann really was a neat person.

"Come on, let's get these scissors back. We have lots to do before the afternoon social with Camp Bigfoot," I said as the screen door slammed behind me.

Robin had been sitting outside on the doorstep. "Your hair looks great, Tracey. Yours too, Nancy Ann. What... what... do you think? T, do you think you could cut my hair too."

We laughed. And turned around to go back into the cabin. Robin followed. Robin had turned out to be a little dynamite.

There was no more room. It seemed like my things had doubled in size since I had first unpacked.

"Try sitting on it, Tracey," said T, laughing.

"You sit on it!" I said back.

"Bambi, how about you?" and everyone laughed.

But I knew my suitcase wasn't going to close. "Nancy Ann, do you have any room?"

"Not really. And I have to be careful. My pressed flowers may get crushed."

"I think it's my dirty clothes. Why do dirty clothes take up more room than clean clothes?"

"Probably because they're not folded properly," said Heather as she placed her last garment into her bag. "Maybe, you could stuff the rest of your things in your sleeping bag. Oh, that's right, you have no sleeping bag. Hmmm... how about a pillow case?"

"Good idea!"

"Has anyone seen my pink hoodie?" asked T.

I looked under my bunk for leftovers. And then behind the door. On a door hook was my baseball cap. I hadn't worn it since the baseball game, since Paul had come into my life. I folded it carefully and placed it in the pillow case. I guess it is okay to put stuff away when they were no longer part of your life. Now with my new hairdo, I would look better without the cap.

I thought about all the things that Nancy

Ann and I had gotten into the past weeks. The days had gone by all too quickly, especially after I had met Paul.

I picked up a smooth river rock lying on my bunk: one of my momentos from the water hole. It was a strangely shaped rock. It was in the form of a heart. I would never forget this summer.

Packing all our stuff and then cleaning up the bungalow for the last time was a set-back. It took us longer than we thought it would. We weren't done till well past lunch time.

We would be ready with a hearty appetite by the time we met everyone. I was having some mixed feelings about saying our goodbyes.

"You almost done?" asked Nancy Ann as she sat down on the floor.

"Yeah, give me a minute."

"Let's put all the bags over by the door and then tomorrow morning we can put our last-minute things inside easily," said Heather.

Everyone except for Candy and Helen followed her suggestion. They left theirs by the bunks.

I won't miss them at all, I thought. But I knew saying goodbye to the others tomorrow morning wasn't going to be easy. And the hardest good-bye was going to be with my friend, Paul. But we would keep in touch by texting and there would be summer camp next year. And Paul. And the rabbit food wasn't so bad once you got used to it. And exercising. I could live with that too, and now I would have to adjust to Big B's not looking over my shoulder every minute. Except lately, she had given up on watching Nancy Ann and me, or maybe, we didn't need watching so much. In either case, life the past few days was a lot easier.

"Okay, I'm ready. Let's go," I said to Nancy Ann as I put my arm through hers. I took a side-glance in the mirror. Pretty nice, I thought. My posture was good too. We were the last to leave bungalow fourteen as the screen door slammed behind us.

Lightning Source UK Ltd.
Milton Keynes UK
UKHW010049060620
364507UK00003B/782